NECROMANCIES *and* NETHERWORLDS

Infinite wrath, and infinite despair?
Which way I fly is Hell; myself am Hell....

—MILTON

NECROMANCIES *and* NETHERWORLDS

Uncanny Stories
by
DARRELL SCHWEITZER &
JASON VAN HOLLANDER

WILDSIDE PRESS
⚜
BERKELEY HEIGHTS, NJ • 1999

Published in 1999 in the United States of America by
Wildside Press, 522 Park Avenue, Berkeley Heights, New Jersey 07922.
http://www.wildsidepress.com

Book design and illustrations ©1999 by Jason Van Hollander

Paperback edition ISBN 1-880448-66-1
Hardcover edition ISBN 1-880448-65-3

TABLE OF CONTENTS

*Dedicated to Mattie, who understands the
need for "just one more book" in the house.*
DS

Dedicated to Terry, who is at ease with all my demons.
JVH

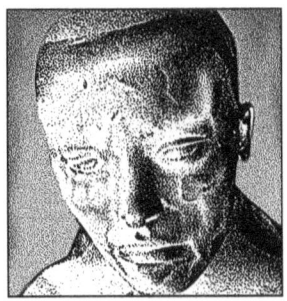

The Crystal-Man

FIRST IT IS THE PATTERNS. In the white, shining heart of the glassmaker's furnace I perceive the beginnings of some exquisite design, patterns, the subtle flame-motifs favored by my master Vaxos; those very zigzag crests which Vaxos engraves on piss-pots, on vases, and most especially on the fantastically intricate funerary vessels so popular among the great merchant-princes of Zhamiir, whereby the ashes of the deceased trickle endlessly through tiny veins of glass, giving the overall figure a semblance of motion, even of life.

There: in the country of fire. I stare into the flames by the hour until my eyeballs are dazzled, seared, fascinated by whatever glimpse I might gain of that bright, unreachable country beyond the burning gates, where no flesh-man can ever pass. There: the rhythmical leaping flames laden with mystery; the parching brilliance leaves my face a cracked landscape, irrigated only by the sparse rivulets of my tears.

There. So beautiful.

Only with the greatest reluctance can I ever draw myself away, close my eyes, rest them for a minute, then regard the duller, imperfect world of the workshop itself. The dark world, the shadows, where the gods are not.

I turn aside. I put down my stoking rod. Elsewhere in the house, Vaxos my master, that colossus who towered over my life almost like one of those forbidden gods I have always sought, lies coughing out his lungs. I hear the barefoot patter of the servant girl, racing to empty a chamberpot before Vaxos coughs again.

They say that the blood of Vaxos boils in his veins. I, who have lived with him for all my life that I can remember, believe it does. Perhaps it hisses in the girl's pot. Perhaps, too, his untreatable disease might be the result of endless experimentations, the new powders and ores whose toxic exudations Vaxos steadfastly ignored.

Or it might have been his temper, his legendary thunderings, whereby at the slightest hint of imperfection, the labor of weeks would be hurled into the street, the unworthy journeyman hurled likewise. Stranger things are rumored, though I have never witnessed them: recalcitrant objects of glass and crystal flogged by the Master of Glass in a frenzy of perfectionism; barrels of potash and lime taken into his own bed so that an unwholesome "chemical coition" might occur.

* * *

Indeed. Back to work. While the furnace heats, the floor needs sweeping of the ash and glittering bits. The pontil rods must be filed clean. So much preparation. Tonight, despite the proximity of my master's death, he is to create his greatest work. All must be in readiness.

Shards crunch under my feet.

* * *

That I had survived at all, and so long, in the service of this glass-frenzied madman was a matter of some wonder to all concerned. It couldn't have been pity. Vaxos was too lacking in human qualities for that.

No, I think it was *utility*. Somehow a wretched, ragged boy showed up on the doorstep of the glass works, who might have been an imbecile or a changeling for his inability to remember any past life at all, this bag of bones, barefoot, burnt from sand and hot paving stones, close to death as he lay parched in the summer's heat, this amnesiac waif blown like a swirl of dust out of the trackless desert, was, in the eye of Vaxos, *useful.* Imagine a tailor walking along the street. He looks down. He sees a chipped piece of wood. To him it is not a scrap, but a button. All it needs is some polishing, some carving, a hole drilled in the center for the thread. He thinks, *Ah! I can use that someday!* and puts it in his pocket, to be saved and filed away, even though the suit he is presently working on doesn't require buttons of that sort.

So it was that the dreadful Vaxos picked me up in his arms. With his own hands he fed me chilled broth, on that summer evening so long ago, at the true beginning of my life – for all I may have been ten or eleven at the time – and with those same hands he bandaged my blistered feet, that

I might be able to walk among the shards and nubbins and sweep the workshop that very night.

So I did.

The following morning, he sent for a cobbler, who made me a pair of heavy boots, and for a tailor, who made me plain clothes of the cheapest, though serviceable materials. Only much later did he remember to give me a name, *Ilvador*, which merely means "what I found."

*   *   *

Why?

My gaze strays back to the furnace door, into the wonderful country of fire beyond.

Passion. Everything that walked or crept is governed by one passion or another.

I close the door, shivering in the sudden absence of heat and light. I resume, and complete my sweeping; then I lay out on the table all those special instruments my master will need, like an acolyte preparing the holy of holies for the coming of a priest.

Dangerous thoughts in blaspheming Zhamiir, where the gods have been cast down in the name of Commerce and sold. But, yes, the passion of Vaxos is something akin to worship and I too care for nothing else in the world but for the beautiful workings in glass and the fires that birth them.

*   *   *

Once, when I was fifteen years old, as Vaxos lay snoring after a particularly strenuous orgy of glass-making – a commission from the emperor involving life-sized glass horses in fantastic colors – I slipped out into the city streets, looking like some automaton in my heavy boots and leather apron, with my hair a formless explosion from countless singeings.

There was so much noise, I thought it must be a carnival. I hadn't been outside of the workshop in years. I had only the vaguest idea of what the rest of the world was like.

It was a carnival of a sort. All around me people cavorted in fantastic costumes, trailing long, colorful streamers. Drunkards swilled and puked on door steps, laughed and swilled some more. A woman danced naked, splattered with mud every time she slipped and fell, to the great merriment of onlookers.

But the celebrations had a more fantastic, serious side, as I found out when I reached the great forum of Zhamiir. There the great sandstone idols of the gods were being torn down and smashed into gravel while crowds cheered, and the more precious silver and gold images were put up for auction. The tapestries and carpets from the temples, the famous cloth-gods, they too fell prey to the depredations of the money-men. On that day you could acquire a fertility deity for a mere half-dozen *royals*. No one was even interested in profit. The revolution had occurred. The merchants had overthrown the gods. The low prices were intentional, to show that the gods were contemptible and impotent.

Woe to any sincere devotee who thought otherwise.

Woe.

As I drew nearer, I saw that the auctions were conducted under compulsion by the priests themselves, many of them naked, their bodies covered with welts and burns, the flesh of their faces and hands flayed off and replaced with ridiculous waxen masks and gloves. Here a weeping dog with the webbed paws of a toad. There a fish whose arm-stumps ended in carrots and celery.

A procession of such wretched creatures passed right in front of me, chains clanking, dung and stones and insults raining down on them. I stood in silent amazement unable to work up any ill feeling toward these holy men at all.

Instead, I began to weep. They were martyrs, suffering for those very gods who had withdrawn from unworthy Zhamiir for inscrutable reasons of their own.

I struggled with the seeming paradox that gods who *were* gods could be driven out by men. I came to no conclusion save that they must have left of their own accord, and would return one day, if mankind adequately repented.

Somehow one of the priests must have been able to read my thoughts. He broke away from the procession and knelt at my feet, staring up at me through a mask like the behind of a jackass. Wax fingers fashioned and painted like congealed masses of cheap coins feebly hooked onto my wrists.

"You are a *miracle*, child," he sputtered. "Yes, you. I think some god reached down and touched you, blasting your mortal life from you, opening you up to new and divine possibilities which only the years will fully articulate. Alas that this miracle has occurred too late! Alas!"

Then someone yanked him away. I saw that his mask had fallen down below his chin and that his face still seemed to be, quite impossibly, burning. Tiny blue and white flames danced over the ruin of his features.

I screamed, but my cry was lost in the laughter of the crowd which closed over me like a sea.

Later, in the silent evening, I came to the cemetery, where the corpses of deceased notables had been dug up and placed in an obscene tableau, murdered priests dressed as rats chewing on the dugs of the late empress who was made up as some kind of serpent-harlequin; near skeletons dancing and gaming and coupling in a parody of life that I, amnesiac Ilvador, whose slate of a mind had been wiped clean by the gods, failed to understand for lack of referents.

I didn't get the joke, but I laughed anyway. I still do not know why. All around me, corpses creaked in the wind. They dangled, impaled on stakes or crucified on the branches of trees. The cemetery remained quiet at this hour. The fun and festivities had drifted to the city's center, in the forum and the despoiled palace, where the emperor was already well beyond ever being able to pay my master Vaxos for the glass horses.

I laughed and danced and joked with the dead well into the night, the infectious spirit of the times having come over me. But then I truly repented, and wept, and begged each and every cadaver its forgiveness, and rearranged them so that all of us were kneeling, facing the sunrise as we worshiped the coming sun and the distant gods.

Thus Vaxos found me. Thence he dragged me by the hair through the sodden, besotted, smoky streets, back to his workshop where he administered a beating of such legendary proportions that the awe-stricken assistants who witnessed the event – for he still had a large staff in those days – spoke of it in almost reverential tones for the years to come. Those who survived, that is. Rumor also has it that Vaxos killed many of his apprentices, or even fed them alive into his furnaces, so that their agonies might contribute unique hues to the glass.

Maybe so. I came to understand then that even as I am the instrument of Vaxos, to be pounded into useful shape, so he, unknowing, is an instrument of the gods, shaped by them to some inscrutable end.

When I stopped screaming, I was allowed to lie down in an ocean of my own blood and dream fantastic dreams.

*　*　*

Vaxos is dying. Cough. Cough. Splat.

I can but struggle to understand. I dip a rag into a bucket of water and hold the rag to my nose, trying to breathe through the sopping cloth. Yes, it must be like that for him.

Trembling as I do so, I put on my master's apron, which is still too large for me, and his own porcelain mask, which he wears to protect his face against the searing blast. The visage is that of a puff-cheeked angel, now sooty, the gold paint of the angel's hair long since burned away.

Thus I become Vaxos. Thus I open the furnace door and peer through his eyes, beholding or imagining some mystical, impossible supernal beautiful face begin to form amidst the flames; and I strain to hear it speak words I cannot even begin to understand.

Thus Vaxos finds me.

"Boy!" He grabs me by the shoulder and whirls me around. He rips the mask from my face and slams the furnace door shut. It is useless to protest that I am not a boy, that I have spent a full twenty years in his employ, obsessed as he, hungering day and night to be taken into his confidence, to know his secrets. "What can you mean by this impudence, except to mock me?"

"It's...not what you think!"

"Oh, it isn't?" Now he wears the mask, wheezing through the round mouth-opening, all the more terrible for the absurdity of the image. Blood splashes over the lower porcelain lip. "What am I thinking? Can you tell me that?"

I cannot. He sags onto a bench and coughs into a clenched fist, under the mask.

"I meant no disrespect, Sir. I did it in order to understand your suffering." I hold up the rag. "Why else would I nearly suffocate myself? Surely not for amusement"

"You are a strange boy," the Master of Glass allows after a few minutes, and in this musing admission I think I detect tones of defeat, a kind of knell. Truly, the old man is dying.

"You know, Sir," I say, surprising myself with my own boldness, "that I could easily overpower you, take from your strongbox all the silver *royals* I could carry and – "

Vaxos waves a hand for me to be silent. "Cease this prattle. You're not interested in money."

I gaze intently into the darkness which hides his eyes behind the mask. "No, Sir, I am not. It is crystal and glass that I live for. I worship the flames, as do you. We are alike, you and I. That is why you kept me by your side, is it not? Vaxos and Ilvador, are two of the same kind."

"Perhaps... More strange words from a strange boy. I think this is why I spared you and you alone from my anger. Surely it can't be for the deftness of your craft or the sensitivity of your soul." He tries to laugh, coughing up bloody phlegm, which drips from his chin. Yet behind this brief, wrenching spasm I think I can discern a genuine smile, maybe even real affection.

"Consider what I have said. Consider, too, that you have no issue, no heirs, no apprentices anymore but for myself to preserve your knowledge and carry it on. Teach me. Instruct me."

And this is where destiny touches us, truly. This is where the gods work their belated miracle, through Vaxos, for all I do not think he even knows the names of the gods, or ever had, even in the days of the *god-madness* before the revolution.

But great things begin to happen. The old man's eyes glisten. His manner becomes animated, almost youthful. "I am on the threshold of wonderful discoveries. There are combustibles of unimaginable ferocity that I have only recently devised. New ways to work the glass, new techniques and methodologies that will usher in an age of beauty...beauty which borders on the sublime. A gorgeous and mystical epoch in which the arts of mankind will finally merge with the sublime."

I am amazed. He sounds like a *theomaniac* after all.

"Imagine if you can," he continues, "poems of glass. Prayers encapsulated in crystalline jars."

"I can imagine fanciful moods captured in graceful forms. I've seen that, worked by your own hands. But prayers?"

"Hear me out, Ilvador. Only a two days ago, when I was heavily dosed with *hanquil*, did these revelations occur to me. In my feverish state, I scribbled my inspirations down. As soon as my head cleared, I discovered, among the illegible scrawls, much which had genuine validity." He reaches up to seize my shoulders, to shake me as if I were still that ten-year-old boy he found in the summer's dust. "The results are astonishing! As soon as the furnace is fully heated, I shall arrange a little demonstration. Little? No, very big indeed, the capstone of my career. But now, I must rest, for my lungs tax me beyond endurance."

He emits a syrupy wheeze and leans back unsteadily against the wall.

"What can I do?" I ask.

He motions for a quill, inkhorn, and parchment. He throws the horn aside angrily, for the blast of the furnace has dried the ink. Instead he dips the pen through the mask, into his own mouth, and writes in blood.

Most worthy successor, I pray that I live long enough to impart my knowledge and my quality. In this transference lay my profoundest hopes.

* * *

At age fifteen, as I lay in the congealing puddle of my own gore, I dreamt this dream for the first time:

Vaxos stands over me, blood-mouthed and smiling. It is night. He raises me gently by the hand and leads me along a beach. The night ocean crashes against the rocks. In the waning moonlight, thieving gulls pluck the eyeless flesh from luminous oysters. The old man, wizened grotesquely, capers like a bundle of sticks hurled in the wind, his clothing all afire, but not consuming him. Sparks trail like meteors, forming delicate script which floats in the air, fading before I can quite read it.

Waves burst against stones. Salt spray, like tears, momentarily blinds me. When vision returns, there stands Vaxos, walking on the surface water like a ghost, marvelously transformed, glowing from within, his body no longer of flesh but of purest, living crystal; a shining man, a being of startling translucence, a veritable lantern, every vein, every artery molten and visible.

Bloodfire. Bloodlight. The innermost, inexhaustible energies of my master Vaxos.

The whole ocean has turned bright red beneath a scarlet moon.

A dark vessel floats near the shore, its rigging faintly outlined in orange flame.

"Into the boat, my boy," *Vaxos commands.* "Come." *Naked, I step into the vessel, and discover that it is composed entirely of smooth glass.*

On that first night, and on many others, I awakened in the dark, suffocating, drowning in that dream-sea of blood, gasping out the name of Vaxos the Crystal-Man.

* * *

Bloodlight. I jerk awake, startled that I have been asleep. There has been an unaccountable transition, as if moments or hours have been snipped from the flailing ribbon of my life.

The workshop is suffused with a lurid red glow. There is Vaxos, towering like a god once more, casting handful after handful of colored pigments into the furnace, muttering magical imprecations behind his mask, oblivious to my presence. Once he pauses to stir the molten mixture within, using a long, iron rod.

I stand at his side, fearful of his wrath, but he greets me almost merrily.

"Ah, *protégé*, the hour of your instruction has arrived. Great things await."

He nods toward the furnace. I peer into the beautiful flames, into the country of the gods beyond them. Beyond some impossibly distant horizon, titan faces rise up like suns.

At this moment I am supremely happy. Now, at last, my master is about to reveal all his secrets. I am fulfilled at last.

There is a loud knock at the door.

I turn around, furious. But Vaxos is nonplused.

"Answer that, will you?"

"Who, by all the gods, would dare –?"

"Gods, my boy?"

I hurry to the door, open it, and in comes a shabby, mournful and tired-looking man of past middle years, whistling some routine, irrelevant tune as if he were delivering bread.

But his delivery is a bit more unusual. The stranger holds up front end of a long, rectangular wooden box. The rear is hefted by a *creature* of some sort, living, yes, but perhaps not at all natural, some botched homunculus scavenged from an alchemist's trash heap: skeletal and mal-formed, naked but for a soiled rag about its loins; skin pustulent, oily, and gray; its hairless head almost pointed, like a turnip. One reddish eye blinks ceaselessly. The other swims in white fluid.

The stranger and his monstrous assistant set the box down carefully on the workshop floor. The creature squats beside it and shits.

Still, Master Vaxos merely turns to me and calmly says, "This is Jaexuma, a vendor."

I presume he means the man, not the other, though in my frenzied impatience they seem the same. "And *what* does he sell at this hour?"

The vendor flashes an ethereal smile, and with great deliberation opens the box, which I realize, even before he does so, to be a coffin.

"At this hour," mocks Jaexuma, "I sell clay."

Already Vaxos is counting out silver half-*royals* into the grave-robber's hand.

"Master, what good can come from this foul commerce?"

"Patience, boy. I do it for art. For beauty. Even as a flower grows from a dunghill – "

Jaexuma pokes me playfully. "Never mind why. It's a living." The gray homunculus whistles in assent. Once more Vaxos is overtaken by a coughing spasm. Money clinks to the floor. Quickly the peddler scoops it up, but Vaxos recovers, and the man can only hold out his hand while the Master counts out the silver pieces and takes back two, which are in excess of the agreed upon amount.

Then Jaexuma does not immediately leave. "I want to watch," he says. This is the final outrage. Once more finding my own reckless courage, heedless of Vaxos or even the homunculus, I haul Jaexuma by the collar to the door and heave him into the street, then stand aside as the monster shuffles after him.

I slam and bar the door, leaning against it in sudden exhaustion, and can only watch as Vaxos dribbles more colored powder over the dead man within the coffin. Then he ladles molten glass over the corpse. Steam hisses and rises, and Vaxos says aloud, as if reciting something, "Alive or dead we are all the same, and in the end all of us are only the cracked and flawed crockery of nature – "

" – and of the Gods."

"Leave piety aside and study the worm if you would know perfection. In decay and dust are we all made perfect and equal," says Vaxos, aglow with the firelight, almost – though I am sure my eyes deceive me – luminous from within, like lantern of flesh.

I cannot understand my master's words. They are mysteries. This is a holy time. I cannot understand, but obey and follow and am instructed, as we shape glass over the dead man, until he is encased, a parody of his living self, this fat, wrinkled old prince of the bazaar set in the posture of an exquisite dancer. As the light washes over him and seems to fill him, he, too, is momentarily self-illuminated. But he is a mere shell. There is nothing inside. The light goes out and the glass cracks.

"It is as I had feared," sighs Vaxos. With a shovel, he smashes the glass corpse to bits and hands me the shovel. I heave the remains into the fiery furnace. The mess the gray creature left on the floor gleams with rainbow colors. My master is alive with fire now.

I watch with fascination as he unstops a tiny flask and measures out grains of white powder into his hand.

"This is the dreaded, powerful, and decidedly illegal drug, *hanquil*," he explains, "which was all the fashion among the decadent aristocracy of former times." He counts out the grains again, for my benefit, picking them up one by one on the tip of his finger before touching them to his tongue beneath his mask. "One grain doesn't do much of anything. Two produce a slight giddiness. Three suffice to cure neuralgic aches. Four temporarily numb all pain and produce a sense of deep seriousness, which is immediately dispelled by the *fifth* grain, which transforms all existence into one vast and inexplicable *joke*. Thus did the degenerate nobles laugh and gasp and laugh some more, sometimes perishing of starvation while they waited for the punch-line! Ha! Ha! The sixth leads to a swift, giddy, cackling death!"

"Master! Wait!" At this point I cannot help but notice that Vaxos has *already taken six grains.*

"Ah, but in the *seventh* grain," he continues, "in that one, yes, the seventh, the eighth, the *ninth*, are all things transformed utterly, all ideals met, perfection achieved, what we used to call the divine apprehended – you can call it what you like, boy; to me it is the summit, the summation of my art, the pinnacle of man's rational mastery over unruly nature! It is pure beauty!"

By this point he has ingested ten grains. He trembles, like a nervous dancer about to begin. His whole body streams with sweat. The facial features of the *porcelain mask* begin to shift, producing a wild grimace, which yields to laughter, then horror, then an expression which, truly the eye has never seen before.

I know it then. The gods are returning, through Master Vaxos, for all he perhaps does not realize as much.

He turns to me, one last time, and says, very sincerely, "It is all so *funny*, my boy, so absurd, and therefore beautiful. The joke is that there is *nothing there*, nothing beyond the proverbial veil, in the empty country of the gods, anywhere. Nothing! Only the furnace is pure, in its utter destruction of all imperfect things!"

Then I watch in helpless horror, weeping like the bewildered child I once was when first he found me and named me, I who am merely That Which Vaxos Found – I watch as the great wizard of glass, Vaxos, rolls and stirs the molten mass within the furnace, as he draws a great mass onto the end of his blowing-rod, and shapes a perfect crystalline skull, as fine a thing as any he has ever produced.

I am left with the irrelevant worry that no one will buy it, since such luxury goods are now out of fashion, bearing as they do the stigma of old-fashioned rank and privilege.

Yet he labors with renewed vigor, with awesome artistry, a magical thing himself, already beyond mere living or mere death under the influence of *hanquil*. But if this demonstration is to be my education, it has failed. I do not comprehend. I beg him to slow down, to explain. He has given me only a puzzle, not an answer, not clarity.

Can he intend that I spend the rest of my days figuring it out? Is he like the father who makes his son heir to a vast treasure chest, then commands him to find the key?

Yes.

At the very end, he does what no competent or even sane glass-blower would ever do.

He inhales through the blowing-tube, and at once the fury of the furnace explodes within his ruined lungs, transfiguring him with fire, with colored salts, with the ashes of the smashed corpse, with the *very light of the gods*.

A human beacon. Brilliant. Consumed. His mask falls off. His face is burning, outlined in tiny blue and white flames, yet his expression is totally calm. He is at peace. He has achieved his goal, even if beyond my reach, beyond my unworthy sight. His body crumbles up like charred paper and is slowly reduced to a smoldering mass of ruin right next to the watery smear of homunculus dung.

I try to convince myself that he looked on me fondly at the very end, as a father on his son. That would be the conventional, sentimental image. But no, he was distracted. I don't think he even remembered I was there.

* * *

What follows is all madness, all hallucination, all transcendent of reason and therefore true.

I rage. I howl. I weep. I shovel the remains of my master Vaxos, along with the homunculus dung, into the ravenous furnace. The air is thick with *hanquil* fumes. The gods appear to me in the fire. I see them clearly, each wearing an exquisite mask of colored glass, their true features too beautiful for any mortal to look upon and live.

And they speak to me. They tell me of the crystal-man who is to come, who is to redeem mankind and lead penitent Zhamiir back to holiness. It is my task to *build* this messiah, here, in the workshop, using the familiar tools of my trade.

And I set to work, fashioning an arm, a torso, another arm, all delicate constructions of spun and blown glass. I hold hot glass in my bare hands, burning my flesh almost through to the bone, but I do not think to wear gloves, for the crystal skull speaks to me in my master's voice, and it is Vaxos who explains to me that only through pain can true holiness be reached. Yes, now, dead and beyond, Vaxos is a *theomaniac*, a reasonless believer like myself, a slave to the gods.

Yes. I am very happy.

Once the serving maid bursts in, sees what is going on, and screams like a horn blasting at some endless festival. I silence her with the shovel and feed her to Vaxos, who devours her hands, so that I can see her fingers swimming in blood inside the crystal skull. The rest I heave into the furnace, stirring her soot and blood and charred bone into the glass.

When I am finished, the naked, gleaming body of the new messiah stands before me, perfectly formed, its muscles smooth, shoulders broad, hands ready to seize the world, glass joints cunningly worked so as to move without any friction.

It lacks only a head.

Reverently, I scramble up a stepladder and place the crystal skull on the massive shoulders. Then, in a moment of whimsy doubtless caused by the *hanquil* fumes, I crown this all off with my master's favorite night-cap.

Silently, slowly, the thing moves around the room, the skull filled with fire now, its mouth whispering secrets from the far side of death, things even skeptical, obsessed Vaxos would never have admitted in life. To me, they are a wisdom beyond words, filling me with an understanding I cannot yet fathom.

Yes, it is like a life-long task to find the key to the treasure-box.

Or to make one.

The door to the street begins to char as the my creation reaches to touch it. Hurriedly, I heave the bar aside.

The *Crystal-man* steps outside. Someone screams. He disperses the darkness of the alley like a rising sun. A company of the watch come up against him. The first man reaches out with his pike, but at the *Crystal-man's* touch both pike and man burst into holy flame and are transfigured.

The others run off, screaming, pikes clattering where dropped.

As the sun rises, we stand in the great forum of the city to greet the returning gods. The *Crystal-man* speaks with the voice of the earthquake. Shutters, flowerpots, and tiles tumble to the ground all around us. The multitudes assemble, and they hear the holy word. *Vaxos* has done this. *Vaxos* has been the instrument through which we are brought into a new age of righteousness and beauty. Through *Vaxos* the world is transformed.

So it would seem, had not *Ilvador* bungled.

As the sunlight fills the square, the light within the *Crystal-man* flickers and goes out. The thunderous voice is reduced to *pings* and a cracking sound, as, indeed, fissures spread through the whole of the glass body, which tumbles to the pavement and shatters into a cloud of brilliant dust.

I am just agile enough to catch the crystal skull and preserve it in my arms.

I am left standing there, trying to comprehend this catastrophe, as the crowd closes around, and there are men with pikes once more. But they remain uncertain, afraid to touch me, and at some distance they convey me into what used to be the imperial palace, where now the Nine Guardians of Public Rationality meet and confer in a great room ceilinged in gold.

I repeat my message, of the coming of the gods, but it is only Ilvador speaking, and the walls do not shake.

(I try to figure it out, as the *hanquil* fumes clear from my brain: some flaw in the glass, some false ingredient; perhaps the mere fact that I never *tempered* what I had wrought, and the sudden temperature change as it was exposed to the cool morning air caused it to crack?)

I hold up the crystal skull as evidence of what I am saying, but my burned and almost useless hands bungle once more.

I drop the skull, and it shatters at my feet, merely glass.

After this, of course, I am helpless and swiftly condemned for violating more laws than anyone can enumerate.

I can only beg that I be burned, that I be cast into the very furnace of Vaxos, so I might join him in the country of the gods, which lies beyond the fires.

*　　*　　*

But they have caused me to be crucified. As I hang on my Tree of Pain, I am not afraid, because Vaxos is with me, transfigured and transformed, a glowing ghost, explaining to me at last that I've gotten it all wrong. I am not *his* instrument. No, he is *mine*. I am the new messiah, the messenger of the fires. I. Ilvador, whom the gods caused to be found on the doorstep in the summer's heat. It was their doing. Their touch wiped out all memories not relevant to my mission.

I.

My heart is a heart of glass. That is my secret. I cannot die. I, too, under the influence of *hanquil* and the divine vision, inhaled through the blowing tube and filled myself with holy fire, with strange, powdered salts, with the soul of beauty, which for so long resided imprisoned within Vaxos.

In me beauty is liberated.

I am the Crystal-man.

Already a day has passed. I greet the sun for the last time. The earth begins to shake.

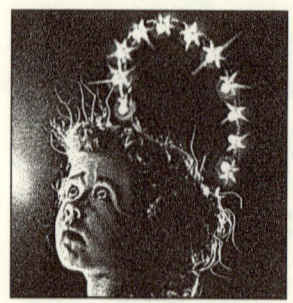

The Cloth Gods of Zhamiir

*LORD YANDI TO HIS NEPHEW, Prince Lebalan, Greetings.
Zhamiir City, date uncertain, in the Year of the Great Awakening*

Beloved Nephew,

What an incredible place! That is the beginning of my explanation, my excuse, if you will – the reason your aged, doddering, and confessedly long-winded Uncle has completed the arduous journey hence, in something resembling secrecy, without even telling you, my confidant Lebalan. Yes, it was urgent. Yes, the greatest secrecy *was* required, for the most astonishing of reasons.

I ramble, I fear.

Zhamiir! The amazing city.

When we entered Zhamiir, we were promptly festooned with reeking-sweet garlands. A thought came to me: *the perfumed corpses of the newly dead, beginning to "go."* It was not quite a pleasant smell. Nothing in Zhamiir is quite pleasant.

Former priests welcomed us at the city gate, professional greeters now. Vendors (former acolytes, says Hesh) swarmed, hawking trinkets, fruits, baubles, chipped and tarnished icons – these latter mere curiosities, no longer holy. Sullen old women (ex-priestesses?) strutted before us in diaphanous costume so we might inspect their dreary wares. And I realized that an entire class has been displaced in Zhamiir. Gone are the priests, gone the temple bell-ringers, the divine seeresses, the ineffably sacrosanct harlots. Gone, all of them, with the introduction of the god-auctions.

"Make way!" the caravan master shouted again and again. He had to raise his stick until a path was cleared. Dizzied by the garlands, we staggered through the granite gate which is the preferred entrance to the famous city of Zhamiir – "where the gods have been subdued," as the new expression goes.

Still the former priests swarmed about us, and my thin-lipped and disapproving Hesh protected his Lord and Master from this beggarly rabble by shooing them away with a big fronded whisk. (Doubtless he was expecting a pipe or two of *hanquil* for his efforts.) I have to laugh, even now, recalling the scene. Hesh is such a droopy, sad clown, as grave as the once-priests themselves.

Throughout our three-week journey he made the most astonishing observations:

"The desert dung-beetles," said he, "have less shame than the slave-deities of Zhamiir. They, at least, roll in shit of their own choosing."

And also: "The sand of the Iracassi, each speck, mocks the vanquished gods."

At a fountain within the city, I ladled sparkling water over my brow, recalling these matchless philosophies. And through this flowing mask, I smiled at the absurdity of all around me. Gods for sale! No more do worshippers make expensive sacrifices in the temples. No more collection baskets. Now gold flows *from* religious observance, not into it. A topsy-turvy world! The thought of it so amazed and pleased me I wanted to dance. The water ran over my ears like a whispery song and I looked around for Hesh, unmerry Hesh.

Soon government clerks surrounded us, thick as flies. Will the Zhamiirites sell off their rulers next? Kings, lords, bureaucrats, the lot? One can only hope.

Many documents were initialed and stamped. Money changed hands. The caravan broke up, the tongueless bearers and their overseer paid off, the camels led away. When it was done Hesh and I sported bronze medallions around our necks, designating us short-term visitors to Zhamiir, *tourists*.

Otherwise we were free. "What's to stop us from going to the auctions this very night?" I asked.

Hesh returned me a troubled gaze, as always when I suggest anything. What a long face he pulled this time! "Bad luck...to purchase a god...so soon into the city."

"Better check their teeth first, eh?"

"Master, this is a serious occasion."

"I am merely optimistic, my dear Hesh. Merely that. It makes me cheerful. Eager."

We proceeded. In spite of his best efforts, Hesh, poor man, could not prevent two guides from attaching themselves to us. Dwarfs, they were, from somewhere in the bazaar, darting out of the tangles of booths and penned animals and barrels and huge jars and jostling crowds. One moment I had merely Hesh, the next, these two with piping voices and rapid little legs. I couldn't refrain from giggling.

"Master!" my servant hissed. "Your dignity!"

Still I laughed, at Hesh's futile cluckings, at myself (I was fairly drunk with fatigue, and with anticipation), as well as the vagaries of nature which fashion such tiny grotesques.

"*Hanquil* dens, down this alley," the big-browed one announced. "Love may be purchased very reasonably here," intoned the other, making obscene gestures with his stumpy fingers.

"Alas," I sighed. "I am too weary."

"Of course," said the other one. "You are well into your years."

"I am a vigorous man!"– I thumped my chest – "Not nearly so old in my appetites as some of the younger men."

"My brother meant no insult," said the smaller dwarf. "You have come to our city for the auctions, I take it."

"Perhaps."

"Ah, a wealthy man," crooned the other, his huge forehead and the hedge-rows above his eyes making him seem all the more ridiculous.

"A collector," chirped the smaller, "a connoisseur, come all the way across the Iracassi Desert to purchase one of our poor gods."

The dwarfs looked at me eagerly, awaiting my response, but it was Hesh who spoke, slowly and deliberately, as if addressing a multitude.

"My master has come to Zhamiir to witness the end of the Age of Miracles. Perhaps he will acquire a souvenir, if it pleases him. A token of the Great Awakening…the time when men are made free from the gods."

"Takes a lot of money to buy a god, even a little one," the big-browed dwarf observed, bowing, before he produced a feather brush and started dusting my feet.

Thanking them, I threw some newly minted coins (one of which the small dwarf promptly bit), then Hesh and I managed to escape.

I paused, further along, taking deep breaths, that I might sample the exhalations of this fabled city.

The streets, Nephew, the streets! What a riot of color before our eyes, what noises, what spicy stinks! Murmurous crowds, low-hanging banners drooping above us, shops, glass-blowers, soul-merchants, stunning women for the harem, the beautiful, honey-colored children of Zhamiir, all swarming before us like figures on a glorious tapestry. For a time I forgot my exhaustion. Merely being in Zhamiir filled me with frenzied energy. After three weeks in the Iracassi, I can tell you, I was grateful for such a glorious vision.

It was twilight. Shadows filled the rabbit-warren streets, softening contrasts. Sounds grew muted. Intricate lanterns swayed on posts as they were lit, one by one, by a spry old man who sang with the purity of an angel.

Here! Here mankind had triumphed over the gods!

The beauty of it moved me deeply, and I felt that mystical-mercantile stirring which is my gift: I felt the Tears of Imminent Fortune rolling out of my eyes.

"Can't we just peek into one of the auctions?" I pleaded with Hesh, dabbing my eyes with my sash.

He took me by the hand and led me. "Bad luck so soon. Consider all things first, Lord, then act deliberately. Your *enthusiasms* are like summer storms, swift and thundcrous and soon gone."

I obeyed him and followed. Sometimes even I forget who is the master and who the servant.

* * *

Sleep, dear Nephew, eluded me that first night. At the place where we stayed, a kind of palace for the wealthy traveler, there was much to keep me awake: sighing breezes, occasional shouts or blaring horns from the distant street, Hesh snoring in the adjoining room, flickers from torch light dancing under the door – and voluptuous grunts that rampaged up the marble halls. This last disturbed me. Almost delirious with fatigue, I flung open the slatted door and beheld the gleaming marble corridor.

In the middle of this hallway I stood, a man of sixty years, half undressed. Then a faint shuffling advanced. A servant appeared, a boy of perhaps ten, thin and terribly frail, with hair as white as the moon.

"Who indulges in love at this hour?" I demanded, nodding in the direction of the sounds.

The boy shrugged at my question. I gazed into his face, into his almost colorless eyes. Something about him fascinated me immensely: his body was all bones and angles and blue veins. He wore only a ragged robe of the same diaphanous stuff the women had worn at the city gate. In the half light, with torches flickering behind him, he seemed somehow less than entirely real, not a solid child of flesh, but an apparition.

I wanted him very much. No, no Nephew, you mustn't think that your old uncle has acquired a new vice. The familiar lusts are enough for me. This was merely the desire to *acquire*. The boy was a treasure. He was beautiful in his strange way, his eyes too wide, his head too large for his shrunken body, his skin like white marble, perfectly smooth, delicately shaped.

He seemed a symbol to me, the final hieroglyph in the mystery of existence. He couldn't be merely a malnourished child. No, that was impossible.

He held a tray, on which were two red, dripping roots. At first I thought they were vegetables, at least. Then it occurred to me that they were bloody claws, torn, not severed, from a bird, probably a peacock.

He placed the tray on a stand beside me. I stared down at it for a moment. When I looked up, the boy was gone. His bare feet had been utterly soundless on the smooth, cold marble.

Repulsed, I emptied the tray into a chamber pot, then stood again alone in the empty corridor. I no longer heard the sounds of passion. There was only silence now. It affected me strangely, this silence. There is a quality, Nephew, about walking in places where men dream. As if in compensation for our dream-loss, we are granted a strange serenity.

Soothed by this very quality, I drifted down a flight of stairs and into a courtyard. There, limned by moonlight, the boy-servant was kneeling, burying something. Ah, but I hadn't meant to spy on him.

"Are you real?" the child asked me all at once.

I wasn't entirely sure. I pinched my wrist and it hurt enough for me to reply, "Yes, real enough." I stifled a yawn. "What a question. Why shouldn't I be real?"

The boy rose to his feet, carefully brushing dirt off his hands and knees, as if to remove anything which might mar his unearthly appearance. "You could be a ghost," he said.

"If the gods are sold in Zhamiir," I teased, "then surely ghosts are given away for free and are found everywhere. You should be used to ghosts by now, and able to recognize one without any hesitation."

He stared at me, utterly unaware of my attempted humor, his eyes wide, bewitching.

"Have you ever seen a ghost?"

"Alas, I have not. In my own country they are reserved for the privileged few. Have you ever seen one?"

"Not of the dead," he said softly, and if embarrassed by the admission, "but of the living."

I asked him to explain what ghosts were.

"Souls without bodies."

"And what are the gods?" *This* question, Nephew, I asked in deepest earnest. My instinct was alive again. Somehow this boy knew. He was an ambassador who moved freely between life and death, my fancy told me, perhaps a native not of this world of living men, but of the other.

"The gods – " he began, shifting nervously. He didn't seem to know. Were he merely a child, I would have concluded that he was simply too young, or too frightened of this strange old man who accosted him in the middle of the night, interrupting some secret doing.

To put him at ease I smiled and touched him gently on the shoulder – his flesh was cold – *cold!* – and quoted one of the old poems of Zhamiir, now forbidden: *"The gods are portions of Eternity, ensouled."*

He stood still, gazing up at me inscrutably.

"Do you like poetry, boy?"

"I don't know, Lord."

Cautiously, I toed the burial mound. "What have you buried here?"

"A peacock, sir. What's left of it."

"Eh?"

"Promise you won't tell?"

"I promise."

"I was hungry, Sir. They mistreat me here."

"It was merely that, hunger? Not some secret divination?"

For the first time, he seemed afraid of me.

"No, Sir!"

"And the claws? What were you doing with them, in the hall outside my room?"

"I had to get rid of them separately."

"Why, of course," I said calmly, pretending to understand. In truth I hadn't the slightest idea what he was talking about. Another mystery. "What is your name, young man?"

"I am called Nimbulec."

I was beginning to feel the weight of my body and my years. I eased myself onto a marble bench and bade the boy sit beside me. Above us in a tree, some night bird chirped softly. The boy sat, shivering.

"Tell me, Nimbulec. What are the god-auctions like?"

"I only know what I hear, Sir. I'm not allowed out."

"And what do you hear?"

"That the auctions take place in a bazaar that used to be a big temple. The gods are rolled up in carpets and the ends are tied so they can't get out."

The child alluded, of course, in his imperfect and beguiling way, to the ensorcelled carpets of Zhamiir, rugs which thump and crawl, gods trapped inside, but not merely bound inside the carpet, but *woven* there. That is the great secret of Zhamiir, Nephew, the means by which humanity has been liberated. The weavers of the city grew so skilled, so cunning with their threads and their dyes and their patterns, that they could create the very, the true likenesses of the gods in cloth. Thus they bound them, snatching each god out of the air when the image was made in a carpet, binding each god when the last knot was tied. There were, there still are, many, many weavers in Zhamiir. With the help of the people, with the backing of rich patrons, they wove many, many carpets, far more than there were gods. They got them all.

I had heard as much during our trek across the Iracassi. The men of Zhamiir had long been tyrannized by the gods and by their wicked priests. They rose up, a revolution led by weavers and rug-merchants.

I sat still beside the boy, thinking, for once unsure of what I was doing in this place. I had been so firm of purpose when I arrived. Now I was getting muddled.

"I should like to purchase a god, Nimbulec," I said. "If I have enough money left over, I should like to purchase you, too, from your master. Do you have any idea what he paid for you?"

"I was a foundling," the boy said solemnly. "A gift of fortune."

*　　*　　*

"This is a gift," I told Hesh later, offering him a vial of *hanquil* and a glistening glass pipe, newly purchased. "Take it," I commanded. "You've earned it ten times over. But, I beg you, please don't puff anything until we return from the auction. I need your mind at its sharpest."

Hesh, feigning surprise, lowered his gaze and held open his wide, dusky palm. "Thank you," he intoned, but joylessly, or else he would not have been Hesh.

We were just finishing our dinner. Servants of the house scurried in and out, deferring to Hesh and myself equally, as if we were not master and man, but two guests of similar rank. I looked around for the boy Nimbulec, but did not see him.

The day had been without purpose and without profit. I'd gone into the bazaar, but found little worth haggling over, only trifles, like the pipe and the *hanquil.* So I had returned to the baths, allowing myself to be cleansed and purged. My beard had been curled too, so perfumed with a volatile pomade that I swore I'd burst into flame if I stepped out into the sunlight.

Dear Nephew, that's how wasted the day was. I was reduced to caring about such matters.

Night would be everything, though, the purpose of our wait, of our wasted day, of the long trek to Zhamiir. With the lowering of the sun, the stone horns of Zhamiir would cry out the triumph of the city, and of man, signaling mockery of the defeated gods. Then the auctions would begin. I waited patiently. My purse was very fat indeed.

Twilight – that superbly evocative hour – had deepened the ruddy sky. It was like blood infused with Divine light, spilled across the face of the cosmos. Thus it affected my mood as Hesh and I trotted toward the auctions.

Even my inscrutable servant's face was given a new hue. He glowed like a man lit from within, a man afire with the stolen emanations of the gods. "The cloth gods of Zhamiir," he muttered as he pushed and shoved our way through the noisy, gaudily-dressed crowd, into the courtyard of a half-destroyed temple, "an entire toppled pantheon, for sale."

A trick of the light confused me: his eyes were dark-orbited pits, pin-pointed each with a single, fiery speck.

I paused, a little afraid. For a moment he was not my familiar Hesh at all, but some other kind of being, gazing out through the fleshly form of my servant as one might through a gauze or veil.

Then I shrugged, dismissing the impression as one more strangeness of Zhamiir.

"The gods. I curse the gods," he kept muttering. I could not get him to explain. I think he sensed something too, that the gods were all around us, not bound in cloth at all, but in the air, in the very dust of Zhamiir.

"I curse the gods," he said.

"Weren't you a temple foundling?" I asked, as we made our way under a frowning, blood-lighted arch. "Didn't the gods protect you? Didn't they protect you?"

"My mother abandoned me to the gods, and the gods abandoned me to the riddle-priests with their detestable chants and their insatiable hunger for money. Not as honest as regular merchants either. They gave no good value for their coin."

"Whereas, if one goes to a rug-merchant to buy, one comes away with, at the very least, a serviceable rug."

Oblivious to my delicious irony, he clutched my sleeve as we halted in front of the desecrated fane. "Don't be put off by the auctioneers," he suddenly warned me. "They are priests, god-smitten men, even now. And they wear masks. While you were gone today, I asked many things of the household servants. They told me that the priests wear masks."

"Masks?"

"Their faces have been burned off. The skin of their hands is peeled off as well. Masks of paraffin and gloves of human skin – their own – to spare the sensibilities of the bidders."

I shuddered. I glanced around at the crowd. The people of Zhamiir seemed tense, filled with emotion waiting to burst forth. They were raucous, but this was not a happy crowd. This was no holiday, but, I felt, a ritual of unending vengeance, against the gods, against the priests, against everything vast and magical and beyond the grasp of the individual Zhamiirite.

"But why these particular mutilations?"

"These were the high priests, the true visionaries, not the petty money-grubbers you saw at the city gate yesterday. These men beheld the gods regularly – not merely the stone idols, but the true, spiritual forms – and they spoke with them. They dreamed mighty dreams and spoke prophecies. They made the people of Zhamiir afraid. Therefore the authorities decreed that they should suffer the most, disfigured, being forced to sell their own gods on the auction block. It is thought just."

The crowd heaved forward. Hesh clung to my sleeve as we passed beneath a cracked frieze. A tiny tile fell onto my head, a perfectly blue square of porcelain the size of my fingernail. I turned it over in my hand as if it were a coin, then slipped it in my pocket.

"What did you find, Master?"

"An omen, probably. Are signs and omens also sold in Zhamiir, along with the gods?"

"No, Master. Without the gods to direct them, the omens occur at random. They are worthless."

"Ah."

The courtyard opened into an inner yard, once the sanctuary of the temple and forbidden to all except the priests. Here, many things drew my attention and wonder. Headless statues turned slowly on circular bases, driven by some unseen mechanism, their stone hands waving slowly in the air, beckoning us onward. Numbered plaques dangled from posts. A huge proscenium held the bundled wares, the very gods themselves, while god-beaters stood guard over them with their flails of gold, whose knouts were barbed with the finger-bones of the faithful.

Even here, hucksters were everywhere. Bags of coins on every counter. A Tabernacle of Commerce.

The crowd jeered. They shouted and clapped hands. They blew on obscenely-shaped wooden horns. And many of them put on masks, the visages of hyenas and rats and serpents. Nearby was one with the face of a drooling idiot, but with a third eye in the middle of his forehead. He was triple cross-eyed.

I asked and Hesh explained:

"Thus they mock the priests, whose scabby faces were burnt off."

The noise rose to a crescendo, then dropped to near silence, as some of the actual priests were herded out onto the stage. I could tell they were the disfigured ones immediately. Their masks were not clownish, but somber, almost expressionless, molded of pale white wax.

The silence did not hold, but gave way to rude shouts from the gallery behind us. Ah, the merriment and torment of this place! Black pigs, let loose from somewhere at the back of the stage, ran squealing between the priests' legs. An elderly priest tripped and fell. His mask shattered, and he sat up. Screams from the stage and from the audience. I glimpsed a raw red oval. Then he was led away, a bag over his head. The pigs tumbled down into the crowd. Small boys chased after them, shoving past the adults.

Lamps swung wildly on poles, agitated by the crowd. Undergarments and pornographic tapestries flapped from pillars like flags. Someone threw a clown mask toward the stage, sending it whirling over the heads of the priests. Another mask followed, and another.

Then a priest raised his hands and there was *silence*. His mask was not like the others. The mouth of it was huge, grotesquely distorted, like that of a painted clown under torture. As if by magic, at a mere gesture from this one, the *tambangs* and *zootibars* were stilled, these musical instruments placed on laps as, meekly, the crowd settled to the mucid, once-glossy marble floor. You could hear the birds of evening chirruping in the trees once more.

"The foremost of all the high priests," whispered Hesh, "once lord of this city."

"A salute to Abannah," the priest began, his voice very soft, but perfectly audible, like the wind. Behind the translucence of his mask, charred lips writhed like worms. He made references I did not understand, to "souls sold in Tamarack," to "the black ship of Ong-Zwarba," and to "Mung and the sign of Mung," and to "Bel-Hemad, on whose shoulders the birds of the air find rest."

Many of his other words were strange too. He spoke the priest-talk, the religious dialect of the city, now preserved only in ribald jokes, and at these auctions. Hesh quickly and accurately translated: "….the tutelary deities of the city…being soft gods, gods that loved their people, gods who did not allow themselves to be feared, even when they were stern and just."

The silence of the crowd turned to anger. I sensed that these arrogant Zhamiirites were still a little abashed at what they had done, that they did not wish to be reminded of how things had been before the Great Toppling of the city's pantheon.

Rotten vegetables flew at the doddering once-priest. His mask was broken by the impact of one of these missiles, and he staggered back, his ruined forehead bare. He crashed into the wooden racks and a single, gorgeously embroidered carpet tumbled into the stage with a thud, then wriggled slightly.

A god-beater stepped forward, his flail upraised, but the priest fell to his knees, trembling, and kissed the rolled cloth with his waxen lips. As he knelt, an assistant gingerly tied a yellow sash around the old man's head, binding his broken mask in place, concealing his seared flesh once more.

"Start the bidding!" the crowd shouted, again and again, making it a chant. "Start! Start! Start!"

"Look," I whispered to Hesh. "The old priest weeps. This is a cruel thing, no matter how wicked he once was."

"He cannot weep, Master. His tear-ducts were burned away."

A wind arose from nowhere, whirled about the former holy of holies, choking us with dust. I felt, for an instant, a presence, as if a thousand ghosts were rushing by, turning, rushing again. I shivered.

"Lord?" a voice from my left side called. I turned, surprised. Hesh sat on my right. For just an instant, the boy Nimbulec was there. I touched him. *Cold.*

"What are you doing here?"

"I?" said Hesh. "I accompany you. To witness this spectacle, and perhaps to acquire a cast-off divinity."

I whirled. "Not you. Him." I turned back to where the boy had been. He was gone. The people nearby gazed with great intensity at the stage, unperturbed.

"What is it?" said Hesh.

"Didn't you see him?"

It was clear he had not.

* * *

The auction proceeded. First the carpet which had fallen was auctioned off. I went to raise my hand, to bid, but Hesh tugged on my sleeve.

"It is never wise to bid on the first," he said, but others did, and the carpet went to a huge black man clad in gold. His fair-skinned servants bore the thing away. I thought I heard the captive god whimper.

Soon I perceived that the pantheon of Zhamiir was a vast and unequal one, and that the hierarchic standing of each god is displayed by the weave and design, as well as sheer yardage. Gods with some significance are sold in bolts of brilliantly-patterned twill, the ends tied with special silver or golden cord. Lesser deities are rolled in cylinders of garish fabric, fantastically patterned. Godlets, demi-gods, demiurges, and the like are wrapped in mats, curtains, or even scarves.

But the prices brought by each divinity were not necessarily relative to the size of the carpets, or the finery. There was a pattern here, which I could not divine. Yes, a loaded word that.

For once I broke away from Hesh, and placed a bid on a carpet rolled long and thin like a snake, and pale green, without any exterior design. That one, perhaps –

But I was defeated.

"No, Master. It was not the correct one for you," said Hesh.

I bid again and lost.

"Nor that. Please wait. Do not throw your money away."

"How does anyone *know?*"

"Perhaps by chance. Much is left to chance in a city not ruled by gods. Perhaps the gods themselves call out to their new masters. Perhaps they manifest themselves, like foundlings on a temple doorstep."

Hesh, strangely, was weeping. Around us the crowd hooted and jeered as each new carpet was brought out, stood on end, and its provenance described.

"A god of hearths and fires," said the priest. "Good for the wife and children. Good for keeping your feet warm in the winter." (Oh! How he visibly winced to make these witticisms! Surely a torturer had written the speech for him.)

Still more gods came onto the block, many crawling across the stage, hunching like huge worms while the beaters whacked them. Strange, glittering dust rose.

"The god-dust," Hesh told me. "The last remnant of the power of the fallen ones. See how it rises like smoke."

Moans emanated from the carpets, like nothing else heard on the Earth, aetheric squeals, the last babblings of the helpless, senile gods of Zhamiir.

Still bids were called out. Plaques on pillars were flipped over to the next number, and the auction continued.

"When?" I whispered.

"I know not. Perhaps not this time. Perhaps never."

For once my precious Hesh was wrong, truly wrong. The time came. I knew it. I had gazed down at my purse, then opened it, peering in at the golden royals within. Then I looked up, and to my astonishment beheld the gaunt, pale boy Nimbulec on the stage beside the priest. He had his hand on the current offering – a plain brown carpet with no markings, bound in ordinary rope – steadying it, as if he were the priest's assistant. No one else seemed to have noticed him. He smiled directly at me.

I leapt to my feet.

"That one!" I cried. "I'll take it!" I offered all that I had, so vehemently that no one opposed me. The priest, startled, acquiesced quickly.

The boy Nimbulec had vanished somewhere.

Still the crowd hooted and gibbered. Still the priest made his painful speeches. But I paid no more attention to the events of the evening. I sat down, contented.

"Have you done right, Master?" Hesh asked. He seemed afraid. He genuinely didn't know.

* * *

"Patterns," Hesh mused as we carried the thumping, wriggling carpet through the near empty streets. "Unceasing repetitions call forth the gods. Chanting will do it."

"Unceasing repetition will also bind them," I said, "as it has in our prize."

"The subtle designs in a carpet, any carpet, even a seemingly plain one, the mirrored strands, the sidereal weft, and" – he paused for a deep breath and continued, most solemnly – "the looms, the worm-driven looms that spin for centuries in incantatory rhythms. All these things the gods confuse for devotion."

"The prayers of the priests," I said, "echoing down the great roadway of time, repeating, repeating – "

"– a thrumming which the gods sense, which draws them, which nourishes them."

The center of our carpet sagged. We nearly lost our grip on it. Hesh struck it underhanded with a golden flail which had come with our purchase – "an added benefit," the priest had said, "for one so generous" – and it straightened itself and even seemed to grow lighter.

"Ah, time," I said. "Vibrations which *accumulate through time* and bring the gods to us, the sigils which draw them down."

So we walked through the dark streets, our speech distracted and strange. I hardly knew what we were saying or what was meant. It was as if some others spoke through the two of us, babbling in their own secret code. But it all fit, like the revealed wisdom that comes to the drunkard or the *hanquil*-addict in his delirium, only to evaporate like a misty dream in the bright morning.

It was only as we reached our rooms that my mind cleared. I began to worry about finances. Had I overspent impulsively? Would we even have enough to pay for our rent and our passage back home? I worried about thieves too, about the long journey itself, about accidentally tearing our own aged guts from the weight of our treasure.

Exhausted, we dumped the carpet unceremoniously on the floor. Hesh fetched cool wine from the kitchen. I sat still, regarding the still form before me. Once it had been placed on the floor, the carpet did not whimper or move. It seemed merely a roll of cloth.

But I knew better. I cannot truly express, dear Nephew, how I felt just then, exhausted but trembling in my final expectation.

I have not made it clear precisely *why* I had come to Zhamiir, why I had done this thing.

I can only try to express it in words. The mere strokes of the pen are not enough. The utterances of the voice are like grains of sand flung into the air by a child trying to cover up the sky that way. Verily.

I think some folk purchase gods in Zhamiir out of sheer self-exaltation. They do it to show that they are greater than gods. How better to show one's own grandiosity than to have a former divinity of field or forest nailed to one's wall or floor? Surely a general would be pleased to furnish his tent with a god of war.

That is one reason. Another is superstitious. People think these fallen gods will bring them good fortune. But this is illogical, even as it is illogical for our own countrymen to believe, as so many do, that the tail of the *hata*-lizard is lucky – for all the good luck that particular lizard enjoyed! Similarly, if the gods had any luck to spare, they would not be in such a ridiculous state.

The third reason is more intimate, more personal, more vague. It is as much a mystery as anything celebrated in the darkened temples of old. There are those who, for all they do not respect the gods, seek the divine, for themselves. What fascination, what uniquely personal glory, to hold in one's hand that which is, or was formerly, divine.

Such persons wish to draw the essence of the gods into their own souls, to gain wisdom, or power, or whatever it is the gods have to offer, to become, in a sense, gods themselves. This is done at a great price, surely, so those who purchase a god of Zhamiir with such a goal in mind take on a greater burden than any weight of cloth. They may despise the priests, the temples, the money-grubbing of organized religion, but they are secretly as god-mad as any whose face was flayed away.

In that way I too am mad, Nephew. Because I am old, because I am near to death, I seek news from that far country into which I will soon journey. Because the gods are immortal, even the gods of Zhamiir, I hoped they could provide me with some glimpse. At the least, they could grant me something akin to wisdom, so that my life might have its proper culmination, like a deal rightly concluded, like the particularly deft final line of a poem. I did not seek immortality for myself, but merely reassurance.

I do not think the people of Zhamiir can understand that, nor can Hesh, nor can even you, my dear Nephew. But ponder it. It is my reason.

Therefore I bought the carpet that I might lie on it, and sleep, and dream, and in my dreams the god within the weave might make himself known to me.

Therefore I waited, breathing hard. Hesh returned with the wine, and I drank. It soothed me.

"Slowly, Master. Slowly."

I swallowed.

"Have we any money left?"

"A little, Master."

"Good. Then I want you to make a second purchase. Now."

"*Now?* What can be so important that you must have it now, at this hour of the night."

"Trust me, good Hesh. I know. Go rouse the master of the house. Then purchase the boy Nimbulec and bring him to me."

It was my intention that Nimbulec should lie beside me on the carpet as I slept, so that whatever wisdom I might gain from the god would be passed on to him, and my explorations of the Beyond would not perish with me. I wanted to make the boy my apprentice in the understanding of Death. I felt certain that he would be naturally talented in this endeavor.

Hesh paused, as if embarrassed to speak.

"What is it?" I said.

"Master, as it happens, when I went for the wine the steward of the kitchens asked me if I had seen that very Nimbulec. It seems the child has run off."

"Then we shall proceed without him," I said, hiding my dismay.

So Hesh and I cut the ropes which bound the carpet and unrolled it, slowly revealing an extremely intricate, albeit badly faded pattern in the cloth.

And something else.

Hesh was the first to cry out.

Then I, too, screamed and fell to my knees, hiding my face with my hands like a priest who had lost his mask. But I looked through my fingers and saw what was there: it was Nimbulec, horribly beaten, his gauzy robe melted into his blood and torn flesh like a huge scab.

For an instant yet he was still alive. He turned toward me. Our eyes met, his glassy with pain. Then his flesh fell away even as I watched, crumbling like grains trickling from an hourglass. His skeleton was fantastically delicate, like a tracery of spun glass, like a spider's web. When it was gone too, all that remained was some dust, and the old, shriveled claws of a bird.

Numbly, Hesh and I unrolled the carpet the rest of the way. In the dim light we could barely make out the overall pattern of the weave. The threads were brown and black, the lighter against the darker revealing the image of a god, who was like a bird with the face of a solemn, gaunt child who stared at us with wide, pain-filled eyes.

I understood nothing then, nothing at all, but I knew what I had to do. I dismissed Hesh for the night. He was reluctant to leave, but I bade him sleep outside my door.

Then I lay down on the dusty carpet and tried to sleep, to call the dreams of the god into my own mind.

As I lay there, my fingers played idly with the shrunken bird-feet until the feet broke like old twigs.

* * *

What followed was not a dream. I am sure of it. It was a true thing, which really happened.

The child Nimbulec sat beside me where I lay. He was naked now. He sat up, out of his ruined gown, passing through it like smoke. I touched him on the knee. Still his flesh was as cold and hard as marble.

I babbled. "My boy, how would you like to come and work for me? My nephew is a rich merchant-prince. We live together in a great house, where there are many servants like yourself, a whole community of them, with children your own age. We work our servants hard, but we feed them well, and there are no beatings."

"And if they are false to you, Master?" said he.

"Then, most reluctantly, we sell them."

"As all things are sold, Master."

"Yes, as all things are sold."

Without another word, he rose and left the room. I sat up, startled, the hurried after him.

Somehow I knew it would be useless to call for Hesh.

I ran. Once I caught a glimpse the boy – a flash of white in the moon-light – as he vanished among pillars. Again, as he turned a corner. Again as he flickered through a doorway, into the courtyard where he had buried the peacock.

Onward, into the city. A waxen-masked priest passed us in the street, singing a dirge, ringing a little bell. I ran, gasping in the suddenly chill night air, reminded of my own mortality. What if my very heart burst? There are physicians in Zhamiir, yes, but I had little money with which to pay them, and there is no charity in a city were the gods are auctioned off. Into the desert. The sands of the Iracassi swirled around us in a sudden storm. I lost sight of the boy. Then the storm passed. The air was clear once more. Now the silence was absolute, even the sand asleep and dreaming.

It seemed that I ran across an ocean of night, a sea of sand, as great phantasmal tides surged around me, as dusty surf boiled around my ankles, withdrawing as waves were spent, drawing me onward, downward, out of the world of living men.

It seemed that glowing skeletons of men and beasts rose and fell slowly in the sand, swimming like fish.

Then I heard Nimbulec, far ahead, singing the priest's dirge.

I came to the top of a dune. Thousands of brilliantly colored birds rose up in my face, peacocks, pheasants, hawks, their wings thundering, like an incredible tidal wave of wildly undulating flowers, flame-colored, paradise-tinted.

Then they were gone, and Nimbulec stood before me, his hands apart, as if he had just released all those birds. I knew that he had.

I heard a voice speaking from the sky. It sounded like Hesh. *"Will we ever recover the gods, recover them truly, and bring them into the world once again?"*

Now shapes like crabs rose out of the sand, but their faces were those of men, and more than men, ancient, inscrutable, implacable.

"Nimbulec!" I shouted.

He smiled when he saw me. He looked up, at star-silvered gulfs. The sky surged like another, incomprehensible sea.

"You will not recover the gods," he said, his voice impossibly loud, inside my mind, "because you have never truly lost them. You reasoned correctly, old man of a foreign country, when you concluded that the dust rising from the carpet was the power of the god bound therein. The gods have never departed from Zhamiir. They are in the very air, in the very dust. The people breathe them with every breath, filling their lungs with miracles."

He walked toward me. Once more I saw that his body was fantastically delicate, his skin a pale tracery of blue veins. The light of the newly-risen, waning moon shone through him clearly, and he cast no shadow.

He took me by the hand, and, yes, his touch was very cold, of the grave.

"Come with me now, and journey into the dark land," he said. "This is the meaning of your coming to the city. Your every act was an omen. Everything manipulated you to this end."

"Master," I said, very deliberately calling him that, this child whom I had once wanted half as a servant, half as a curiosity the way one might collect strangely-shaped shells. "Master, at the end, at the very end, I find that I am afraid."

"Come," he said. "Leave your fear behind like an old cloak."

Naked, I ran beside him, my body young and vigorous as it has not been in thirty years. I ran, down a gray slope of ash, down, out of the world, through those gates through which the dead souls pass, down into the other land, where the souls of my ancestors rose up out of a marsh to greet me, where a black castle filled the sky and the few, strange stars were the torches flickering in its windows; down, past the great dragon that waits, down into the swirling chaos, into nothingness, which is neither darkness nor light, neither thunder nor silence.

And all the wisdom I ever sought and feared came to me, and all the glory. I had reached the end of my curiosity, of my fascination.

* * *

But here is the most exquisite irony of all, dearest Nephew. I had never died. Not quite, not yet.

Shortly before dawn Hesh disobeyed my order and came into the room. I don't know what he saw exactly, but in sudden alarm he dragged me off the carpet.

I awoke later in the sickbed where I now lie. I am filled with pain. My mind is dimmed, like a lamp guttering out. In my lucid intervals, between pain and delirium, I am able to write.

I cannot describe what I saw. Not truly. All I can say is that, indeed, the gods of Zhamiir are everywhere, in the air I breathe. I exhale miracles and revelations. The vulgarity of the people here, the lewdness, the anger, the mockery – all these things are masks, like the waxen masks of the priests. Beneath them are the mutilated, god-burned, god-crazed folk of the city, who have magnificently, foolishly, incredibly torn down the hierarchy of the gods, spilling the divine power out of the temples where, in other lands, it is safely contained like boiling pitch in a pot. In Zhamiir men have been scalded by it, every last one of them.

* * *

Hesh enters with fresh pens and parchment.

"Write if it comforts you, Master," he says. "I fear you may not last long. The strain of the running was too much for you."

"The running? How do you know about that?"

"I had a dream, Master. I saw you go."

"A dream sent by a god, a revelation?"

He will not answer that. I cannot ask him about gods and men, about the land beyond life, about the strange ocean in the desert.

I ask what has become of Nimbulec.

"That is very strange, Master. The innkeeper says that they did have a servant boy, who killed a peacock, was beaten for it, and ran away. But he was not like you described. No one has seen a child like that."

"What happens now, Hesh?"

At the end he is like a parent to me. I seek comfort from him. I long for his constant strength.

He is deeply moved, for a long time, unable to speak.

"Master, when I found you, I listened to your heartbeat. It is weak and irregular."

"And the gods are only drawn by a steady beat which never varies. Is that it?"

"I think so, My Lord Yandi."

Ah, Nephew, my heart burns like a torch in my chest –

Men Without Maps

"**I** HAVE BEEN A SOLDIER ALL MY LIFE," Jyrim said. "Truly, all of it. It is the doing of the gods. When I was very small, the people of my village cursed the gods and refused to respect the divine. The altars were overthrown, the priests slain. But I was too young to understand that. I only knew that, perhaps sent to re-instill some of that lost respect, the pestilence came. Everyone, my parents, my brothers, everyone in my whole world died of it. The crystalline sickness. They stood still that last morning as the sun rose. They continued to ridicule the gods, all the while gleaming in the morning light, their faces, their naked bodies – for in the last stages of the disease, of course, the sufferer is tormented by bodily heat and so is often found naked in the end – and they just stood there, as I am sure they stand now. But I could still walk. I did not gleam. Naked, though, I ran out of my world, across the plain, into the unknown vastness. Soldiers found me. At first I thought they would eat me, but they adopted me instead, and raised me as the son of the whole regiment. So I am one who had a thousand fathers and no mother. For I was reborn that day and became, to the exclusion of all else, a soldier."

The old man settled wearily into the dust, leaning against a fallen column. Around him, the temple ruin was still, open to the bright sun.

"But you no longer wear the sword and the plume. You are no longer a soldier." The old woman sat wearily beside him.

"I have lectured too much. My misfortune has made me pedantic. Tell me of yourself first."

"You are no longer a soldier," she insisted. Her white hair stirred in the faint breeze. Out across the desert, dust devils rose, danced.

"I was mustered out because of my age. I am cut adrift. Utterly."

"You have your pension."

"A pittance. Gone."

"I too am not what I once was," she said. "I too...." She paused and leaned over where she sat, tracing with her finger in the sand. Then she straightened up suddenly and continued speaking. "We are well met, we two. I, also, am sure the gods are responsible. Even here, in godless Tamarack, where men have no more use for the divine. Instead, they serve commerce. But when I was a young girl I dwelt in this temple. Nay, ruled over it. I was the pythoness."

"And now?"

"My snake died. No one brought me another. Therefore, prophecy ceased. I think that was what people wanted all along."

"And I still have – " The soldier reached behind the pillar and lifted out an almost hairless, blind monkey by the scruff of the neck. It glared at him, its eyes pink and puffy, its skin a sickly gray, streaked with purple veins. The creature screeched, snapped. "Yes, yes, I know," the soldier said. He took a piece of fruit out of his travel bag, chewed it, and gave the pulp to the monkey, which ate greedily, nipping his scarred fingers, relishing the drops of blood mixed with the fruit.

"A magical creature," the woman said.

"A nasty, filthy, mean-spirited one. But, yes, magical. That first morning, as I wandered naked over the plain, I encountered this monkey. I reached out my hand to it, and it bit me, then spoke in something other than words. I knew then that it would accompany me always, that I must never allow it to come to harm. I had no idea why."

"And you still don't?"

"Oh, it served me well enough. Every time it bit me, for the price of a little blood I was granted a vision, some foreknowledge of my foes' armaments or strategy, or just where the next meal was coming from. It kept me alive. I don't doubt that. But now, since I am no longer a soldier, those visions likewise no longer come. We are useless together, the two of us."

The monkey finished eating and crawled into the travel bag, searching for more fruit. Jyrim yanked it out by the tail. The creature hissed, turned, and bit him viciously on the forearm. Blood flowed. Resignedly, Jyrim let the monkey lick its fill.

"Has this marvelous creature a name?"

"Joot. It is called Joot. If that ever meant anything, I've long since forgotten what. A nonsense noise."

"Jyrim and Joot. What a pair. Come here, Joot," the old woman said softly, cooing as if addressing a beloved child. "It is destiny that we are here today." She held out her hands, lifted the monkey's own, and the creature came to her in a kind of dance. To Jyrim the soldier she said, "I have waited many years for this."

"If you want my monkey, take it," he said, too numb of mind to even be astonished.

"Oh no. It stays with you, but on this day I shall deliver my final prophecy. I need a magical animal to do that. When I writhed, wrapped in the living serpent, the dreams of the gods filled me with fire. Now, with this monkey in my lap, perhaps I can rekindle a single coal."

Jyrim watched the dust-devils.

"You shall travel but a little ways," she said. "I, not at all. Yet we shall both arrive at the same place."

"That's it?"

"I've been out of practice. Besides, the gods have long-since fled Tamarack."

"Explain then." Unthinking, he reached into his bag and got out another piece of fruit and offered it to her.

The prophetess sighed. "You don't need to reward me. My reward is that I may die now, tonight or tomorrow, having prophesied one last time. You, I foresee, shall become a soldier one last time. That is all I see."

"Then I die too?" Jyrim laughed bitterly. "The grave is the place we both shall come to. I could have told you that. Behold, I'm a prophet myself."

The monkey Joot sniffed the fruit, grabbed, and bit, nipping Jyrim's fingers again.

*   *   *

He left her sitting there in the midday sun. The temple ruins offered no shade for anything larger than a scorpion. There was no reason to linger. Throughout the afternoon he trudged slowly across the Zydar desert, away from godless Tamarack, bound he knew not where. The monkey led him. Blind as it was, it seemed to know the way, scrambling across the dunes, its worn leather leash trailing in the sand.

The dust-devils writhed like the serpents of prophecy, but spoke not.

In the evening, the sky darkened to blood red, then purpled, then faded to black. The sand was their bed that night. Jyrim and the monkey lay down near the base of a dune, out of the wind. Jyrim thought to light a fire, for warmth, then realized with chagrin he had nothing to burn and no way to start a fire anyway.

Joot laughed, exposing jagged, blackened teeth.

"Show some sympathy for an old comrade," Jyrim said. "Just this once."

The monkey made a particular barking sound which meant it wanted food.

"Very well then." Jyrim reached into the bag. He swatted his hand against the inside of it, startled. The bag was empty.

He merely lay down. The monkey found its way to him and cuddled in his arms, as if for warmth, then, as if it had forgotten something, broke free and bit him on the elbow.

"I am bleeding all over our bed," Jyrim said, only half awake.

How old was this little animal? He wondered. It had been with him…sixty years? Was that it? Surely Joot was, as the pythoness had discerned, a supernatural monkey, attached to him for some obscure reason. Now that the food was gone, now that he did not even know the way to the next city, now that he had utterly failed to make a living in Tamarack.

"Can your monkey do *tricks?*" everyone demanded. No, it could not, or would not. It merely snapped –

Now he would wander but a little way, lie down even as he did now, and die. Not much of a prophecy. An interesting paradox, though. The woman said that without a magical creature, be it snake or monkey, she could not prophesy. But with the monkey in her lap, she made no more than a commonplace guess. Yet the creature *was* magical. How else could it have lived so long? The visions. She had said he would be a soldier once more. That didn't make any sense. But then, prophecy never did…. It was something to hope for, though. More than anything else, he longed to resume the profession of arms, if only long enough to die, so at least he would be *someone* and not just refuse.

*   *   *

The monkey woke him in the middle of the night, tugging gently on his ear with its teeth. Abruptly, he sat up. Joot's unseeing eyes were wide open, fixed on some distant point in space.

"What is it, old companion?"

Above, stars gleamed in a pure band of fire from horizon to horizon. The Pathway of the Gods, it was called, brightest in summer, dim in winter. There were no gods now. They had fled Tamarack, unappreciated, useless, even as he and the monkey were useless. Odd, that he should find himself pitying the gods.

It could be worse, he told them in his thoughts. The gods of Zhamiir were actually *sold at auction* to curiosity-seekers from far and wide. All over the world, men rose up and shrugged off religion like an old coat.

"But I am an old man and shall retain the out-of-date fashion," he said aloud, to the night air. "I shall be guided by the stars, each of which represents, we are told, a mile we must traverse in this forced march which is our life."

"March no farther. Die. Only die!"

He looked up, startled by this other voice. A giant of a man in a plume-crested helmet and black armor stood on the top of the dune. He knew that voice, that form. It was Agiros, the Zhamiiri champion he had slain in the pass before Great Bull Mountain, thirty years before. That had been the proudest day of his life. How both armies had roared when he stood up from the dust, covered with blood, the head of his foe dangling from his upraised fist.

Now that head seemed to be back on Agiros's shoulders.

"Are you a ghost?"

"I merely am."

Bewildered, Jyrim rose and climbed to the top of the dune. He stood before Agiros and said, "If you are a restless ghost then, I beg you, forgive me for slaying you, and find your rest."

Agiros spat. "Coward. No soldier ever apologizes for killing – "

"– any more than he apologizes for breathing," Jyrim said, concluding the proverb. "So be it then. Have you come to fight?"

Metal rasped. Agiros drew his sword. Jyrim merely knelt, to allow Agiros to strike off his head. He had no weapon. He was too tired.

The sword thudded into the sand in front of him.

"Pick it up and fight. Or else give me the monkey."

"What?"

"I shall tear your little beast limb from filthy limb. I shall grind its foul flesh between my teeth, which is no more than the monster deserves. I am sure the thought has crossed your mind too."

Now Jyrim had a weapon – and strength. He rose in rage and charged his opponent, who had somehow armed himself with shield and spear.

Jyrim shouted. He slashed wildly with the sword, staggering, coughing, gasping for breath as the cold night air tore his lungs. His enemy toyed with him, never allowing him within striking distance, tripping him with the point of the spear.

And Jyrim lay very still, his eyes closed but for a slit, more listening than watching as Agiros approached.

"Dead already?" Agiros prodded him with the spear.

Much of soldiering, he repeated to himself again and again, is not brute strength but strategy. The essence of strategy is knowing when to wait.

Agiros prodded him with the spear, then put his foot on Jyrim's chest.

As quick as a striking viper, Jyrim grabbed the spear and jammed the point into his foeman's calf. Agiros let out a bellow, but before he could even fall, Jyrim had rammed his sword upward, into his enemy's groin. When Agiros fell, it was silently.

Jyrim laughed. "Don't you remember...? That's how I did it the first time I killed you."

But there was only sand, a formation atop the dune which vaguely resembled the fallen giant. Wind quickly effaced it.

A dream, then? No, it was not that. The sword of Agiros was still in his hand, and quite solid.

He called down to where Joot still lay in the sand.

"Come, comrade. Our destiny is upon us. Come."

The monkey did not rise. Bewildered, afraid in a way he could not explain to himself, Jyrim hurried down the dune. He tucked the sword into his belt and picked up Joot. The creature was still warm.

For an instant, he almost wept. The reaction surprised him. Then the monkey stirred, ripped open one of the scabs on his forearm, and lapped his blood.

"Yes," he said. "Refresh yourself. Our campaign is not yet over. You are welcome to my meager provisions. Yes."

*   *   *

Bewildered, delirious with expectation, with a kind of madness, Jyrim staggered across the dunes, trying to follow a star, then putting the monkey down and following its random meanderings.

"Tomorrow, when the sun rises," he said, "we shall roast our brains, you and I. Let us have our last adventure tonight then. No time for sleeping now! No! Sleep all you want when the lizards play among our bones."

Destiny in the billion stars, he thought. The gods walk the gleaming pathway yet! I am led by the blind eyes of a brainless monkey. So be it!

He shouted, waving the sword of Agiros.

He bellowed a camp song he had learned that very first evening. when the regiment adopted him.

"We march to the fight! March to the foe!
March into blood! March into death!
Blood of the fallen! Staining our boots!
March like the thunder! We don't give a damn!"

Everything was suddenly hilarious. His laughter was a soldier's laugh now, a hearty roar to raise his spirits before some terrible battle. Let it be that, yes.

Then, just as suddenly, his laughter sounded like a foreign language, and he forgot everything, even who he was. He sat down again, in the darkness beneath the stars, and sighed.

The monkey scrambled into his lap. He scratched the creature gently behind the ears.

"Why do you stay with me, old friend? What ineffable mystery do you represent?"

*   *   *

The phosphor-man found him next. Gleaming, like a skeleton delicately constructed of wind-borne embers, this newcomer beckoned, then led him for many hours of silent, deliberate march through the Zydar Desert while above the Pathway of the Gods wheeled slowly through the sky.

He came to a military camp. There in the desert, the remnant of some ancient massacre, stood broken walls and huts, overturned wagons, and even the remains of tents. It was all years, even centuries old, but the desert had not managed to erase it.

Appalled, he allowed himself to be led through the gate. He held the monkey in his arms now, the sword still in his belt.

Then he saw the corpses: a bemedalled skeleton in a uniform he recognized, even if he could not remember if it was that of friend or foe. It hardly seemed to matter now. Yet the problem turned in his mind, over and over.

The skeleton still held a curving sword in its bony grip. Nearby, a standard-bearer actually stood, his shriveled remains somehow supported by or entangled in his standard which was still rammed upright into the ground. The image on the standard was, ironically, that of a crowned, possibly divine monkey.

Bones and military tunics littered the ground, half buried in sand; here a shattered breastplate, there a cloven helmet, again, a broken spear. He supposed that the victors had carried off most of the still usable material.

Above the bones were shimmers of light, and night drifts, sand-borne on the faint wind, struggling to gain form. Phosphor-things like great wading birds with human faces stalked through the camp, knee-deep in the sand, graceful, silent, almost totally transparent. All was vagueness: feeble breezes whisking dusk into the sky, into the clouds. Clouds sailed backward into the waning, just-risen moon.

Ghostly trumpets blared. Just as suddenly, the phosphor-man broke up into thousands of individual sparks, scattered, and was gone.

And the dead rose, the skeletons coming together, bone unto bone, sinew rejoining sinew, flesh reconstituting itself out of the dust. They stood up on their feet, an exceedingly great army, while still the trumpets sounded; thousands in the darkness, filling the camp, their eyes gleaming like stars.

He knew them all, every last one, as men he had slain over the years in countless battles. So many, he thought, sacrificed to the trivial result that I should survive long enough to die in the sun with my monkey tomorrow. Ah, the ways of the gods are strange, he told himself. But he despaired: No, the ways of randomness, of a world without gods, like a ship drifting with no one to steer her, *those* ways are infinitely and hopelessly strange.

Men without maps, he thought, wandering hopelessly across a barren world, a place devoid of the miraculous. For the gods had been driven from Tamarack, and had been sold at auction in Zhamiir. Here the temples were made the haunts of lizards.

The resurrected host advanced in step, took another step, and another.

Joot screeched in fear and climbed onto his shoulders, clinging to his neck. It was clear to him now. This monkey was the last fragment of the numinous left in the world, the last miraculous thing, tawdry as it was, and the envious dead would take it from him, would tear it to little bits so each could have a desperately desired, yet useless piece, which would not nourish, or heal, or restore.

So he fought them throughout the night, shouting his war cry. He struck off a leg, an arm, a head. With many a straight thrust he pierced breastplate and ribs, and bones clattered to earth over his forearm like a little avalanche. A desiccated skull fell at his feet, snapping. He snatched off its helmet and put it on his own head. He took a shield from a fallen foe, and once, while his enemies milled about in seeming confusion, he actually managed to strap a breastplate on over his ragged clothing.

All the while the monkey screeched and clawed as his neck and bit his ears and face till blood ran down his cheeks. The temptation was almost overwhelming to cast it away, to smash it underfoot in the fury of the moment, so he could get on with the fighting undistracted. But time and time again he reminded himself that he was fighting *for* this monkey, to carry out the commands of the divine monkey, which had first been given to him on that plain so long ago, as he fled naked from the death of his world. He must preserve the monkey. He must aid it on its journey to no destination he could ever discern, for no purpose he could ever understand.

Yet that purpose was enough. A soldier followed *orders*. He followed *orders* where before there had only been random, senile misery. He felt almost young again.

Foes fell before him like wheat before the reaper. He remembered all his old tricks, old moves, old tactics. This opposing army was lost. These men were indeed without maps, without direction or purpose, but he, at last, was not. Despite their numbers, he had the advantage. He thanked the absent gods. He even thanked Joot.

At the very last the few survivors cried out in a single voice and vanished like smoke in the morning wind.

As the eastern sky lightened, Jyrim stood amid the ruins, once more a confused old man. Even the corpses of his fallen enemies were no more than suggestions of shapes in the sand, soon erased by dawn's breath. But, again, it had been no illusion. He still held Agiros's sword in his hand. He wore a dented helmet and a breastplate so tarnished with dirt and old blood it was almost black.

Bleeding from many wounds, he fell to his knees, then lay back against a fallen pillar. His blood splattered on the sand.

It was impossible, he told himself. He had gone nowhere at all. This was the temple of the pythoness, not a ruined camp.

He felt a special pain at the base of his neck and reached back. An arrow was embedded there, in the muscle. He couldn't get the barbs out, and so broke off the shaft. Only then did he discover that this arrow, loosed at him from behind, had impaled his monkey, which hung dead, spitted on the shaft like some small game animal ready to be roasted over a fire.

He wept, deeply and truly, as he cradled the dead monkey in his lap. His tears mingled with his blood and fell on the little, distorted, bug-eyed face.

The prophetess knelt before him. She took the dead monkey into her own hands.

"So is my final prophecy completed," she said softly.

"I don't understand." He gasped for breath, swallowed, tried to force words. He watched his blood spreading over the hard-packed sand. He was very weak now. "Was it some kind of dream?"

"It was foretold," she said, "and in the foretelling, what happened, happened, the future condensed into a single instant of time."

"Have not hours passed, the whole night? Did I not leave you in the daylight?"

But she only sat beside him, sighed, closed her eyes, and stopped breathing.

"Wait!" he shouted. "You can't just leave! What is this supposed to mean? Explain yourself!" Angrily, he shoved her on the shoulder. Her body toppled.

"Hush. Ask no more questions."

He started, jerking his head up at the new voice. The arrowhead embedded in his neck stabbed painfully.

The thing which had been Joot the monkey crouched in his lap, drinking his blood from where it oozed from behind his breastplate as if from a broken fountain. The little beast was alive again, but changed almost beyond recognition into something that might have been a small, deformed child diffused with holy light, so that it was both grotesque and ineffably beautiful at the same time. As he watched, the apparition grew in size and stood up before him, became as tall as a man, but not at all human, its face that of an ape, its eyes burning so brilliantly white that he could not look upon them. Still his blood stained its chin. Flaming wings spread from the pale-white shoulders. A tail, twitched behind, stirring the sand. He somehow found the presence of the tail very reassuring.

He spoke softly, without astonishment. "You are a god."

"I am, yes, concealed in that embryonic form you knew until the fullness of my time was come. Your life has been but my birthing-pangs, old soldier, faithful companion. Even as other lives shall be for many more. Even as men overthrow their old gods, new ones arise in secret. It is the way of things. Gods rise out of the black depths like bubbles in a pool."

Jyrim tried to force himself to his feet. He reached out. But the pain was too great. He fell forward, face-down in the sand, then heaved himself onto his back.

"That's not right," he gasped. "No. *Liar!* Men called you forth, out of their own desires! Yes. *We* created you in the image of our dreams – "

"It hardly matters. Your task his done. Your deeds, your thoughts, your courage, and your blood have all nourished me. Now I shall leave you, even as a young serpent leaves its shattered egg and never turns back."

"Wait! What is there for me? What reward?"

"Haven't you been rewarded already, old soldier?"

"Have I indeed…?"

The god reached down to touch him beneath the chin, like a parent fondling a child.

The light was blinding once again.

* * *

Slowly, his vision cleared. He felt as if he were rising on a cloud. The sensation was all too familiar: dizziness from loss of blood, from exertion. But then he stared into the sunken, tear-streaked face of the pythoness.

Somehow, it all seemed hilarious to him. A cruel joke. He laughed to bury the pain. He shouted the old soldier's song: *"March! March into blood!…March!…Don't give a damn!…Tear down the cities! Smother our foes!"*

"Soldier, will you take me with you this day into paradise?"

He didn't understand.

"Will you…let me march with you?" she said.

"I - I - Into paradise?"

"Come!" Something about her voice had changed, become less raspy, less harsh. He saw that she had become a young girl in the first flower of her youth, that her hair was dark as the night sky, that her skin was gleaming, olive, almost translucent. Something shriveled and worn lay at her feet.

"Come!" she said again. She took him by the hand and pulled him up. It was so easy, rising up, as if he were laying aside a huge, heavy cloak. She held his hand and started to lead him over the sand, toward the rising sun.

But he lifted her in his dark, strong arms, held her firmly against his golden breastplate. His sword clanged at his side, his shield against his back. He felt the wind ruffling the plumes of his helmet.

He shouted a great shout and ran, carrying her, laughing, toward the vanishing darkness of the night, where lingered the army of the lost, the men without maps. They served no gods. That was their problem, he realized. They were leaderless.

But they were his comrades now, and no soldier ever deserted his fellow-soldiers. He would show them the way.

The Caravan of the Dead

IT IS JALLA THE UNREAL who brings me the news, that same idealized projection of my younger self who has wandered far and enjoyed many adventures all these years while I have lain immobile in the sand. Here I am buried up to my chin with an foot-square cubical tent of cloth erected over my face, while he wenches or fights dragons or hunts treasure. Whatever. For this at least he should be grateful, and show a little courtesy. But he does not. He is smug, as I was at his age.

"Give it up, Old Jalla," he says. "Come out of your grave for what little time you have left. Uproot yourself, you desiccated stump. For, lo, the gods are toppled in Zhamiir, and men have tumbled them down, breaking up the marble images for souvenirs, handing over the sacred tapestries to be sold to rug merchants. Even in holy Zhamiir, the mobs, led by the merchants, have flayed the faces from the priests. They force them now, maimed, wearing masks of comical and humiliating visage, to conduct the auctions. Clearly we are living in latter days, O seeker, and your quest is ultimately useless."

The Unreal lad also thinks he can wax eloquent, and he is not wholly mistaken, but he has an exaggerated opinion of his oratorical abilities.

He tugs open my tiny face tent, reaches in, and tweaks my nose. I sniffle, then blink. He crouches on the sand atop my buried chest, his bare toes digging in. I cannot feel the weight of him, though.

He strikes me as genuinely beautiful in the pale morning light, a flower of nascent manhood, clad in the brightly colored, almost diaphanous robes of a nomad of the Iracassi desert. The skin of his exposed arms gleams like polished wood. He is wearing golden armlets he must have acquired since his last visit.

His face, too, is olive-colored and gleaming, beardless. His curly hair

48

catches the first light of the coming day.

"Wake up," he says. He smiles. I think he is going to laugh at me for having spent decades buried in the sand. It does, admittedly, seem ridiculous, I suddenly realize, but only to materialistic and foolish youth, which cannot comprehend spiritual values.

But I am glad for his company. Behind him, the sky has already lightened to that steely blue it attains briefly before becoming white-hot with the furnace of day. It is a good time. I have returned from my nightly spirit-journey, and am rested.

"Old Jalla," the Unreal boy says once more, almost serious. Is there a trace of compassion in him now? I should count it among my many accomplishments. "All I've told you is true. There are no gods anymore. People have turned away from the holy things. What you're doing here is hopeless."

"Harumph..." I mutter, spitting out sand.

He is almost weeping now. I am amazed. The smile was false. He is, in his heart, deeply sad. Who can read him more astutely than I?

"Another day, and still perfection is far off," I sigh.

He traces some inscrutable symbol into the sand over my chest. I feel nothing.

"Bugger perfection," he says. "That is what I have come to tell you. You will never find your way to paradise now. You will never join the company of the dream-walkers. The invisible people have withdrawn from the world."

"But they are the elect, the exalted masters, the ascended ones. In their infinite mercy they wait for us, to take us to the gods."

Jalla the Unreal sits down atop my chest with a thump which I can only feel where the sand touches my cheeks. Often, in my years of lying here, I have wondered if somehow my buried body has dissolved like an old, dead root, till only my head remains like a tree about to be blown over in the wind, kept alive by the drug *hanquil*. There is nothing in my experience to discount this theory. Such are the mysteries and miracles of this truly amazing substance. *Hanquil* alone allows me to remain here. *Hanquil* has made the boy Jalla possible when mere nostalgic dreaming could not.

"I'm afraid that they're going to be waiting for a long time – " he says.

"So they have waited, young blasphemer! So they shall!"

"Because no one seems very interested anymore –!"

"Off! Away! Unreal! Unclean! Unholy!" I try to heave my body up through the sand to toss him aside, but nothing happens. I grit my teeth, grinding sand. Very slowly I breathe out. "Everything you say is impossible. No more than idle fancy, the dream of a dream."

"I am Unreal, and therefore more widely traveled than a man of flesh. I have journeyed far, and I tell you, yes, in all the lands that rim the Iracassi, men have spurned their gods. In Gaboran, Varnos, even in Tzaleshtos where torture is considered a sacrament and the government has previously been most zealous in its pursuit of holiness. Even there, anger, selfishness, worldliness, have fomented risings – "

"I deny this – "

"If you can't accept the word of the Unreal, who can you believe?"

He has a point. There is a long silence while the sky brightens.

"I shall dream on this."

"Do so, then."

Already the blinding face of the solar god has risen above the world's edge. Jalla the Unreal's face and bare arms gleam like polished metal. Then he seems less and less substantial, like a stick figure with a ragged robe flapping in the breeze, and is gone.

*   *   *

But I cannot bring myself to dream. I am so amazed, so angry. I am unable to release my thoughts to rush swiftly, smoothly toward the dreamlands, in the words of the poet Ynas, "as the tide over wet sand." Not now. So I argue with myself.

Ridiculous. Jalla the Unreal neglected to close my tent flap – there were still limits to the boy's good behavior – so now I am staring at Holy Andramzhinos, Lord of Fire, straight in the face, and he is staring back, much to my discomfort. Abandon the gods? Might as well ignore the sun, the wind, the great rivers of the world, for all these things are gods or manifestations of gods.

Jalla the Unreal, I decide, must be mad. He represents some deep craziness within myself which, thankfully was purged when I created him. The desert is full of such ghosts, created by men who seek to be holy. *Hanquil* and holiness working together give them a kind of life, a pseudo-existence neither material nor entirely immaterial, like the wind made flesh.

Poor boy. The defecations of my mind have malformed him, for all his obvious beauty. He is a foolish, flittering creature, like a butterfly on a breeze, with no strength of will. *He* would never have the patience to lie here for half a century buried up to the chin, with a miniature tent over his face, hoping to cleanse himself of all fleshly evils, so that the unhindered inner light might shine forth like a beacon, so that we too – all members of our little community who lie thus – may become ourselves ascended. *He* will never join the ranks of the invisible people and enter the lands of the gods as freely as a householder walks in through his own door.

He'd probably call that selfish, self-indulgent, and useless. He'd tell me to get a job. He, the Unreal. What could he know?

* * *

I hear footsteps approaching over the sand; the most familiar sound in all my existence, that particular gait.

Anaxos the dwarf notes the open tent flap but merely shrugs. He places a damp rag over my face, and instantly my whole existence is filled with the sweet fumes of liquefied *hanquil.* Such ecstasy. For these few instants every day I am reminded I still have a mortal body, and am glad of it, although such a burden doubtless impedes me on my spiritual journey. So great is the power of *hanquil,* even in the minute proportions of Anaxos's solution.

("It's like beating yourself on the head with a brick all day," Jalla the Unreal likes to say. "It feels *so* good to stop!" "Out blasphemer! Ignorant boy!" I hiss back. We have this argument often.)

Hanquil always brings me back to earth. With the rag over my face, I hallucinate visits to brothels, to eating-houses where one stuffs oneself with thousands upon thousands of rare delicacies, which the attendants ram down one's throat with a plunger. I dig my hands, trembling, into chests of coin and jewels, as uncountable wealth streams through my outstretched fingers. I dream of horseback races, of wrestling, of my own young, muscular body locked against another in a delirium of sweat and heat and dust and scented oil. And I dream of war too, of the thunder and terror of battle.

Then Anaxos removes the rag and silently drops it back into his bucket. He affords me a single spoonful of plain water from his gourd. More than that I know better than to ask for. Anaxos is incorruptible. He'll ladle camel dung on the face-tents of any who try to bribe or cajole him.

Therefore I question this stalwart of truth on that which is troubling me.

"Have men really overthrown the gods?"

He doesn't respond. Perhaps my voice has become so ethereal he cannot hear. Perhaps, like a surgeon, he is used to having semi-conscious, drugged patients babbling at him and has learned to ignore it.

"*Is it true?*" I scream. I try to rise. Miracle of miracles, the sand beneath the dwarf's feet stirs. I shall never know how many years of spiritual progress are thrown away in that instant, but it seems worth it.

"What?" Anaxos is clearly startled. The ravings of the dream-mad god-seekers are not something with which he ever expected to concern himself. How mysterious his mind must be. He, too, is kept alive by *hanquil* amid this desolation, perhaps for centuries. Yet he is bound to earth more firmly than those of us who are planted in it, a humble water-bearer, unable to set a single foot on the path to enlightenment.

"Well? You heard me?"

He scrambles back, wide-eyed with amazement. "I really don't know, Master. Overthrow the gods? How ridiculous, but..."

"But *what* you venomous toad?"

"But, it must be admitted, exalted Sir, that the pilgrims do not come to this place like they used to. It has been..." He counts frantically on his fingers. I think he has twelve, no, thirteen. His short stature is, if the expression may be excused, the least of his peculiarities.

"I await, thou ridiculous Oracle..."

"Six months since we had anyone at all. Master, the collection coffers are empty. In time, I fear, we shall even have difficulty maintaining the supply of *hanquil*."

"Leave me."

He scuttles off. More absurdity. In the good times, pilgrims come by the thousands, wading gingerly among the tiny city of face-tents, awed and amazed to be in the presence of such Seekers, questioning us to learn what wisdom we have yet attained. They leave the collection bowls over-flowing with coin. Ours is the most famous of all such sites. Here men are buried all across the face of the desert, and up into the foothills of the ragged mountains beyond, where a few stragglers like myself lie among gravel and boulders. No one in six months? I have to laugh. I search among my ancient memories for the secret of the act of laughter.

So passes the day in some befuddlement. Then comes evening, the magical hour of our emergence. Then the spirits of those who lie in the sand rise up out of their bodies. We pour like glowing smoke out of our own inert mouths – the sensation is like leaving off a heavy, confining cloak – and stand up among the little tent-town, or among the boulders, or on the ridges of the hills. We gather, we engage in small conversation, like caravaneers waiting to assemble, for so we are, in our dreams, as we trudge in a long line over the dunes, far, from where our bodies lay, toward the ineffable dawn of paradise, to the gods. Every eye scans that unworldly horizon for a speck of light which is not a star, not the lantern of some mortal wayfarer, but the gleaming crystal mask of an Ascended One waiting for us, assuring us that, at last, it is no longer necessary to return to our buried bodies.

Many are the wonders of the night, many the lands long dead, long lost to Time, through which we venture. Great kingdoms, now dust in the waking world, rise up before us, and our little band of wanderers passes through gates of cities which knew the footsteps of the very gods and trembled with the thunder of the titans in the first years of the world.

Jalla the Unreal is beside me, laughing, running like a small mischievous child in and out of the column. His energy is boundless. He plays and tumbles with his companions, ghosts created by the minds of other Seekers, as they, too, shed the dross of worldly thoughts. And the spirits of the truly dead are among us too, mournful, rattling like old leaves in the wind, they who gave their lives to this journey and continue on it still, but hopelessly.

I know that when the time comes, the ghosts will leave us, and we will behold the kingdoms no more. Then we shall burn like the rising sun with pure, inner light and come into the country of the gods.

So we journey in the darkness this night, our caravan stretched across the darkened sands like some subtle serpent, barely visible, writhing gently from side to side.

Some of our number ride imaginary camels or horses or even wholly fantastic beasts. I feel that is a vanity, and will impede the unburdening of the spirit, so I walk, feeling the chill wind blow through my thin robe, the quickly cooling sand almost frigid beneath my bare feet.

Night and sameness. All is darkness and the featureless dunes. But above – ! Rich hints of Mystery color the heavens. The prophets warn of the troubling wonder of the Iracassian sky, "which throws magic down on the dreaming sands." So Mystery pours down on us. We bathe in Mystery, swim in it, drawing ever nearer to the shores of paradise.

In the darkness of the night, then, I approach another of our company, one Pyxos, who had been a merchant once but had gone bankrupt and despaired of material things. Thus his misfortune turned out to be his greatest fortune, setting him on the path to enlightenment. But early in his stay among us, he had not been so sure. Often by day he and I would shout back and forth among the stones, up and down the slopes of the foothills, arguing theology, preoccupied with imponderables. He is cured now. If I can take any credit for it, I am that much nearer to the Dream Walkers and to the gods.

This night he rides on something like a huge, golden grasshopper with the face and bare breasts of a woman. He lean forward, reaching down to fondle those breasts, his face buried in the creature's scarlet, silken hair.

"Friend," I ask him. "Knowledgeable companion…?"

He stirs and looked up. "Oh, it's you."

"It is I, the humblest of all seekers…"

"What do you want?"

"Answers."

"Isn't that what we're all here for?" He returns to fondling hair and breasts.

"I have heard such a terrible rumor that the mere thought of it troubles me more than I can account for."

"And what might that be?"

"That the gods are overthrown by men. That the images are pulled down. That all holiness is cast away, and that, therefore, you and I seek it in vain."

"Don't be ridiculous…" He will say no more, and gradually I fall behind him, reassured by his very scorn at such an idea.

* * *

And again an inconclusive night yields to a complacent day. We return, ever more reluctantly, to our buried bodies and rest through the day. Anaxos, once more, services each of us with water and with *hanquil*. He has no more news. He does not respond when I try to address him.

It is as he places the drug-soaked cloth over my face that the extraordinary idea occurs to me. I blame the *hanquil* for the temptation, for the blasphemy if you can call it that, certainly for the *oddness* of what I am about to do.

Passive no longer, I am resolved on a distinct course of action.

I start chewing on the cloth. The absent-minded dwarf seems more intent on picking lice out of his own malodorous hide. Soon my tired jaws and worn teeth have actually torn away a small section of the cloth. I hide it under my upper lip.

Anaxos wanders away. The *hanquil* dreams come with more vivid intensity than usual, for I have ingested every last drop that was in that cloth, rather than leaving some of the precious stuff to evaporate in the sun. Sensual dreams go on for hours. I am rolling like an anchorless ship in stormy seas of flesh, in dark whorehouses beneath faint, swaying lanterns. It is hardly edifying or spiritual.

And, under my lip, I have stored some of the drug for later. I am fully aware that scrap of cloth could slide down my throat and choke me. Even amid the orgy there is a detached part of my mind which worries about this. But it is as if a council of my various selves has been held, and the reluctant are made to abide by the consensus vote. Even young Jalla the Unreal. He is there, listening, his eyes wide with anxiety. He says nothing.

We know what we must do.

There are, indeed, no pilgrims today. Anaxos the dwarf must be asleep somewhere. My neighbor Pyxos makes no remark as the amazing thing happens –

Chewing on that scrap of *hanquil* flavored cloth, I feel I can do anything. I rise up out of my grave *by day*. I casually shrug my flesh aside, and there I am, a daytime ghost, spirit alone, squinting in the brilliant light, gazing down at my own face-tent. I dare not look inside. One never does. It is the true-death to behold your own mortal face from outside your body.

Onward. My spirit is in great pain, as if I have walked into a roaring furnace. But I am not consumed. In time, I can see by daylight.

Onward. Across the plain amid swirling curtains of sand, and the bones of great beasts which dwelt here long ago, when the land was fertile, before the gods scorched in the course of one of their quarrels.

Cast down the gods? Ignore them? Rubbish. I am off to see for myself.

Daytime revenant that I am, I do not tire. Somehow I cover an amazing distance in a short time, for somewhere in the deepest recesses of memory there is the fact that the great city of Zhamiir is at least four days' march away. Possibly I remember that from my own youth, when I was initiated into the order of Seekers, and brought out of the city into the desert to be buried.

The white domes and walls of Zhamiir rise before me, as inevitable as mountains, as fantastic in their way as the lost cities I visit in my nightly journeys.

I join a vast caravan of the living – of shouting men, of squalling children and tittering women, of fat merchants gaming and gambling and counting money in the privacy of their wagons, of cursing muleteers and camel-drivers – all this very material, living flesh pouring like a river through the broad gate of Zhamiir. I am not sure if I am visible to them. After all, I have never done this before. But never mind; they are too preoccupied with themselves to notice one more tattered old man among them. No guard demands to see my pass or papers.

It is a festival today, so I gather. All around the great square of Zhamiir booths are set up beneath gaily-colored canopies. Jugglers and acrobats perform. A giant on even more gigantic stilts wades through the crowd, dressed as a fantastic bird.

And the aromas! More seductive than the fumes of *hanquil*, the smells of meat and pastry and fresh fruit.

I search under my clothing and realize I have no money. I realize too that I haven't had a square meal in longer than most of these people have been alive. Verily, I enjoyed a light snack when their grandfathers were babes…there is no recourse but shoplifting. I reach for a spice-bun, for all its glazed surface has captured the desert's dust and not a few flies. To my amazement, the bun actually moves, but the shopkeeper merely snatches it back irritably, never aware that he was nearly robbed by a ghost.

Again, puzzlement. Did he fail to see me, or just not bother? Am I real, or unreal, solid or immaterial? I think of the boy Jalla, the wind made flesh. I've never been certain than anyone can see him but for myself.

The mood of the crowd suddenly changes. They are filled with vicious anticipation, like a mob about to witness a beast-fight.

To my unending horror, I discover that everything Jalla the Unreal told me is true. Every word of it.

Trumpets blast. The crowd parts. The giant on stilts is nowhere to be seen. A cohort of the city guard forces its way into the square, and in their midst are, exactly what Jalla described – the flayed priests with their masks like laughing pigs and sorrowful dogs, the defiled images, the holy tapestries to be sold to common rug merchants.

I cannot bear to witness the actual auction, and flee, deeper into the city, until I come at last to a many-pillared, marble edifice, the great temple of the many gods. I knew this place when I was a young initiate, and I always delighted in its serene interiors, its tinkling fountains, the soft and perpetual chanting of the acolytes in remote alcoves.

But this, too, has been defiled, raped. The beautifully carven ivory gate, with its thousands of tiny figures, which used to be accounted one of the wonders of the world, is merely gone. Inside, the dome which once bore the sacred mosaic images of every god known to mankind has been whitewashed – *whitewashed!* Utterly erased!

It seems only as an afterthought that the temple has been turned into a cattle market and is ankle-deep in dung.

Weeping now, I arrive at last at the place dearest to me of all, that tiny maze-like garden behind the temple where the vision first came to me when I was – what? – seventeen years old? – which set me on the course of my life. There I will sit again, and listen to the birds and the wind in the trees and surely the sanity of the world will be restored.

But the garden has been shorn. Baled, dead flowers lie in heaps, fodder for the cattle, no doubt. Everything beautiful in this place has been totally destroyed, every statue, the tiny fountain, anything which might incline the mind toward holiness. All is bare stone, bundled flower, and rubble.

It is only after a long while – after I have been hearing moans for a long time – that I realize that what I first took to be mere posts, possibly the stripped trunks of trees, are in fact *stakes* on which priests are impaled, still clad in their finery, the reliquary-chains of their office still dangling.

Most are long dead, their faces covered with masks of swarming flies, but the chief priest is alive still, not impaled but crucified, his body heaved up over the top of a giant wooden *T* so that his chest is toward the sky and his head hangs down behind.

Somehow, incredibly, he is able to turn his head and look straight down at me as I come up behind him.

I blink, and stand there, amazed and ashamed.

"You can see me...?"

"I am near enough to death. Yes. I can see ghosts."

"I am not truly a ghost, Holy One, but a Seeker..."

"Then I pity you, for if you have not found your way to paradise by now, I doubt you ever shall... Get back to your grave. You have nothing left to do but die there."

Once more I weep aloud. I can see the priest is moved, even distracted as he is by present circumstances.

"No! No! Holy One, I *shall* come into paradise, and you with me, by my side. I shall lead your spirit among the Invisible Elect and present you to them as a holy martyr – "

"That they know already," said the priest. "Can you not see them, the shining ones, the invisible people, all around us? How many they are! They fill this garden! Can't you see them?"

"I cannot. Help me! Help me to see them – !"

"You are asking *me* for help…?"

"Yes! I am unworthy! I have been distracted by carnal dreams, by cynicism, I – "

As if in reply he suddenly begins choking – it is his death-rattle, and a great gout of blood pours from his mouth. I deliberately place myself underneath it, thinking to be cleansed in this outgushing of a genuine martyr. But the blood passes right through me and stains the sand at my feet. I can only stand there sheepishly, like an embarrassed and not very bright servant who has just spilled the punchbowl at a party. I see no Ascended Ones, no invisible people in crystalline masks, no gods, nor even the departing spirit of the priest; only corpses and flies and baled flowers in the ruined place that was once a garden.

* * *

It is Unreal Jalla who rescues me at the end. I wander for hours amid the twisted streets, viewing the horrors of the city gone mad, shouting in a voice wordless and ineffectual as a sudden afternoon breeze that barely stirs the dust, proclaiming dire prophecies of the chaos and death and utter desolation that must inevitably arise from the abandonment of all that is holy and beautiful. But the people are drunk with wine and with what they think is their liberation and do not hear me. They do not see me, even if they can.

Folly reigns supreme!

Then the boy Jalla takes me gently by the hand – I am too dazed and numb to wonder how he found me, but I guess it must be some inherent affinity which acts like a pigeon's homing sense – and leads me out of a little dung-gate (how appropriate) into the desert again.

"Old Jalla," he says. He too is clearly weeping. Superficial as his awareness is, I think he has grasped the magnitude of the calamity more thoroughly than I. "Old one…*Father*…" I start. He has never called me that before. It must be even worse than I thought. "Come back. Come now. I need you. It's all ruined now, all lost. Everything. I don't know what to do. Help me."

I touch him gently on the head, as one would comfort a small child. It seems to help.

In mere minutes we are back at our encampment, and I see that once more he speaks only the truth. He is, after all, an idealized version of my boy-self, and somehow I have taught him not to lie.

The first thing I notice is the pall of black smoke overhead, next, its source: a heap of supply wagons and tents, dead camels and human corpses, all smoldering, half-burnt.

I wander through the community of buried ones, unable to count how many face-tents have been snatched away, how many heads lopped off like harvested cabbages. Here and there a stake has been driven through a buried chest, and arms and legs stick up through the sand in a final paroxysm of outrage.

"Why?" I ask at last. "Who...? Couldn't they just leave us alone to rot uselessly? We were already buried? All we had to do was *die*...."

"Marauders, Father," young Jalla says. "Nomads. They saw the place was no longer visited. They figured no one protected it. They came looking for money. They were very angry when they didn't find any. Anaxos tried to explain, but – "

We behold Anaxos the dwarf, stuck atop a spear, very tall in death, turning slowly like a forlorn weathervane. The look on his face is one of helpless amazement.

"No one will avenge them," I mutter. "Let the nomads take Zhamiir too."

"Men of the caravan! Comrades!"

We both turn in astonishment at the sound of this voice. It is my erstwhile neighbor Pyxos, staggering among the desolation – not the ghost of Pyxos either, but the very flesh. He still wears his torn, rotting initiation robe, which has been buried in the earth with him these many years. Pyxos, who has risen from his grave *still alive*, Pyxos whom the nomads must have overlooked where he lay up the hillside among the boulders; my loquacious neighbor Pyxos now waves his arms and launches into a vast oration as complex and beautiful as those stolen marble temple-doors of Zhamiir. I am ravished by his words, as he urges us on to seek the gods, to overcome all petty and temporary setbacks, to breach the very gates of Paradise. I am sure he can see the Ascended Ones around himself now. How familiarly he talks with them, as one would to one's family at table.

Fortunate Pyxos! Surely now his eyes are open to holiness.

"He is completely mad," whispers the boy Jalla, who is after all Unreal and less appreciative of the finer things.

Fortunate Pyxos!

How reverently he lowers the dead dwarf from his undignified perch. Together Pyxos and I and even young Jalla form a funeral procession for our late and loyal servant. We place him in a beautifully-fashioned marble coffin, which inexplicably the nomads did not bother to carry off. We lower him down inside the coffin, into a bath of blue liquid.

"Pure *hanquil*," Jalla the Unreal explains. "It is forbidden to the desert folk. They fear its visions. They were afraid to even touch its container."

"Rightly," says Pyxos, apparently aware of us only now, for the first time. "For is not *hanquil* the source of all human wickedness and woe?"

I sputter, unable to refute this new absurdity.

Jalla the Unreal puts his hand on my arm and says gently, "Pity him. He is mad."

But I cannot pity him. I am trembling with wrath as the three of us work together to dig a grave for the dead dwarf.

The labor continues. Somehow, the longer I am in spirit form, the more I am able to manipulate solid objects. I could barely move the sticky bun back in the city. Now I heave handfuls of sand into the air. Is it because I am dead now, or at least dying? Is my body mutilated like all the others, back where it lies among the stones? Or is it because I am the ghost of a *living* man that I have such strength? Even filled with rage, even distracted by labor, I am of such a speculative turn of mind –

Is it perhaps that the blood of the martyr has somehow sanctified me after all, and what follows is a kind of miracle?

There is no question that Pyxos can see me. But then, his brain is soaked with *hanquil*, as is mine. He is used to phantasms.

Nevertheless, some change has definitely taken place. It may simply be that my grief has given me form and substance, and I shall be stranded here forever like a haunter of old houses, with the power to howl and hurl small objects and bang shutters.

We lower the coffin into the hole, Anaxos bobbing in his bath of *hanquil*. Only then does it occur to anybody – to Pyxos – to find the lid and put it on.

We begin shoveling with our hands, burying the coffin.

"Let it be covered completely and forgotten," Pyxos says. "Let all of it be utterly forgotten."

Then all is clear to me. Enlightenment comes. I stop shoveling. Young Jalla also stops, following my example.

How mistaken I have been. Pyxos is not holy at all. He is, as Unreal Jalla suggested, completely mad. But I cannot forgive him, even so. My anger has hardened into a sharp point.

"Without *hanquil*," I say slowly, "the caravan will never reach the gods. We need this supply more desperately than ever now."

"Anaxos slept thus when he was alive. That was how he maintained himself, pickled in the stuff. Look where it got him."

"He was an instrument of the divine!"

"That and a heap of camel dung will get you a heap of camel dung."

I stand up in my rage. I strike him with my fists, solidly enough it seems to me, but ineffectually. He barely flinches. "Have a care Pyxos! You blaspheme!"

He stops his work and looks up at me. "I am just tired. I have wasted a long life. Now I just want peace and quiet. I want to be free of lies. So, let all lies be buried here. Help me do it, if you were ever my friend."

"*I am not a lie!*"

He sighs. "But you are, poor Jalla. You are a ghost. When the world has rid itself of *hanquil*, no one will see ghosts anymore. When we are sober, delirium fades. You are unreal, Jalla. Soon there will be only the real."

He means me, old Jalla, but his words have clearly wounded young Jalla, my living dream, who cries out as if he has been beaten. I am truly afraid of Pyxos now, afraid that I, and the gods, and all the spirits that haunt the desert will truly fade away when men like Pyxos have prevailed. Was this not the process I witnessed in Zhamiir?

Almost weeping, desperate, my voice breaking, I try to assail his logic.

"Pyxos, you are arguing with your own hallucination. Can such a paragon of rationality as yourself indulge in such foolishness?"

"No," he replies. "I am ashamed of my present state. But once my mind is completely aired out, cleansed of *hanquil* fumes, I am sure I'll stop doing it. You cannot change the situation, Jalla. There is nothing you can do. So please, will you help me bury our small friend here?"

Young Jalla looks helpless. He shrugs. Our eyes meet. He is troubled, looking to me for guidance. I am the boy's father now, and a father must protect his son.

"Nothing I can do, eh?" I shout. "Nothing I can *do*?"

"No, nothing. You are a figment of my *hanquil*-soaked imagination." Pyxos goes on shoveling.

"Well, how about *this?*" I run a short distance away, snatch the very spear on which our beloved dwarf died, run back, and drive the spear through the would-be rationalist's back, until the point protrudes from his chest.

Pyxos merely gasps a feeble, "Oh," and tumbles down into the grave, onto the coffin. He struggles briefly. Blood spreads over his filthy gown, and he rubs red-stained fingers together in incredulous disbelief.

Unquestionably, I have gained the ability to manipulate material objects. That makes me more than a figment. Surely this is clear, even to stupid Pyxos.

I want to shout in triumph, but my anger melts away, and I sit down by the grave, weeping.

"Forgive me, old friend," is all I can think to say.

"The apologies of illusions are not necessary. Where there is no reality, there can be no guilt." So says Pyxos as he dies, embracing the coffin of the dwarf.

Young Jalla and I mourn for him for a long time. We would have enjoyed the company of such a stalwart in the long years to come, but it is not to be. We finish burying him, and Anaxos, right as they are. But first, I find a hammer and chip away a corner of the coffin lid, then take a piece of metal pipe about five fingers in diameter – I only guess its original function, possibly the chimney of some sort of stove – and slide that down into the coffin, into the precious *hanquil.* Then we complete the burial. When we are done, I test my artifice, lowering a flask down the pipe on a string, drawing out *hanquil.* Young Jalla and I raise the flask to our lips, drink. Is it possible for such beings as ourselves to feel the effects of a drug?

It seems to be.

*   *   *

My purpose is clear now, and that purpose is denial. I deny the faithlessness of men. I spurn their wickedness. I have come too far on my journey to turn back now. Unlike poor, sad Pyxos, I have not lost my way. Instead, I have found it. Thus I make some small recompense for my follies, my former errors.

I must lead the others.

Evening is the sacred hour of emergence.

In the evening, beneath the purple sky, the ghosts of our slain comrades rise from their graves, disheveled, mutilated, angry and afraid. Young Jalla and I do the best to explain things.

Hours pass as we redistribute such heads we can find, placing them beneath face tents. We brush away scorpions and beetles, drive off the last few crows which have come to feast. There are many petty quarrels. ("No! That isn't me! I was more handsome!" "No, I had a beard!" "No! I was a woman, you dolt!") But in time, all is straightened out as well as it is ever going to be.

Truly we are the caravan of the dead now.

We wander across the night-shrouded desert, circling, staggering over dunes, attended by spirits, by fantastic beasts, by dreams, as the sky and the stars pour mystery onto the cool sands. Paradise has never seemed nearer. I think the invisible people move among us now, the Ascended Elect, about to become visible. This is our faith. For this reason only, we journey onward.

And each morning we return to our graves. The spirits of the caravaneers fade with the sun. Young Jalla and I alone remain above ground. Then we dip the flask down the metal tube and draw out *hanquil.* The blue liquid has blackened as Anaxos rots, but this only strengthens the effect of the drug.

We work earnestly, the boy beside me a boy no longer, but a mature man, as firm in his purpose as I. We two move from grave to grave, gently placing *hanquil* soaked rags over the decaying faces and bleached skulls. One of those faces might be my own. I no longer care. I have no memory of dying, but as one gains in merit, as one nears Paradise, that sort of thing no longer matters.

My condition is a fading irrelevancy. For this I can only thank the dwarf Anaxos, whom I wrongfully abused so many times. I can only ask his forgiveness now, and hope that he will await for me in the country of the gods.

*　　*　　*

I am the new Anaxos now, only taller. It is fitting. I would have it no other way.

Verily: once soldiers of the new emperor find me wandering on the fringes of the Iracassi. They can see me quite distinctly. They hurl taunts and lies, calling me a filthy, *hanquil*-sodden old lunatic.

A decurion sniffs my rags and pretends to stagger, while the men laugh.

But one of them, a strong and handsome man who could be my younger self, dares to ask who I am.

"Jalla the Twice-Unreal," I reply, "water-carrier for the caravan of the dead."

And I walk between his fellows like a wisp of swirling sand, and leave them.

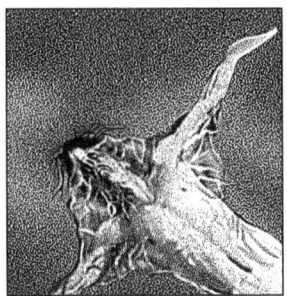

The Unmaker of Men

"**G**ET *UP*, YOU FOOL!" my Master hissed, kicking me hard in the ribs. At the sight of the dread Thulisquar, the Grand Physician of the Ministry of Pain looming in his full ceremonial regalia, his embroidered robe glittering and flashing in the dim candlelight, his black hood swallowing his face; at the sudden appearance of this all-too-familiar apparition my lady of the evening squealed and rolled under the bed, dragging a sheet after her to cover her nakedness.

Likewise naked, I lay on my back and stared straight up at him. I laughed hysterically.

"Boy, you are a disgrace!" He struck me across the chest with his riding whip. I didn't even raise a hand to shield myself.

That was funny too.

The lady under the bed whimpered. Thulisquar ignored her.

Convulsed with hilarity, I rolled onto my side, weeping with ineffable amusement, and also from the *hanquil* fumes.

My Master reached down and picked up the vial of the precious drug from where it had fallen. He held it up to the light and shook it.

"Five grains, eh? Just five?"

"Yes!" I said, finding words at last. "Yes! The common, trivial five!"

More laughter, even as Thulisquar struck me again with his whip, on the buttocks and across the back.

The granular form of *hanquil* is ground from the spiny barbs of a sky-colored fish, I told myself, lecturing on and on in my mind, for suddenly I felt very – ha! hah! – weighty of thought, somber, learned – and it was time for the expostulation of secret lore. *Hanquil* is well known to the physicians and to the decadent elite of Alquaziir, its properties curious and consistent: Three grains suffice to cure neuralgic aches. Four temporarily numb all pain and give the user a deep sense of seriousness, while an additional fifth transforms existence into an excruciating joke for several hours. Or, perhaps one should say, as the seriousness of the fourth grain yields to the giddiness of the fifth, that one suddenly perceives true reality. Our blinders fall off.

Hence the term "five-grainers," applied by the merrymakers of Alquaziir to themselves as a kind of code, a password, a talisman. It is the beginning of *hanquil* addiction, which leads, inevitably they say, to the sixth grain and a mad, laughing death.

Which somehow seems worth it.

So funny!

"Child, you disgust me! Get up!" (Whack! The whip, somewhere.) "Cover yourself! Show a sense of shame!" (Whack! Whack! The prostitute under the bed shrieked in sympathy, then began an endless, gurgling laugh.)

He grabbed me under the chin, so hard I began to choke. (This itself seemed incredibly hilarious.) He stood me up in the candlelight. "You are, what, Ganzeric?" he said. "Eighteen? You should be an intelligent, responsible young man. I have brought you up to be such. How extremely disappointing."

He let go and I flopped down unto the bed. ("Oomph!" said the lady underneath. So humorous, that sound.) I clung to the bedpost, trying to sit upright, but lost my grip and fell back. Once more I lay, still naked, staring up at the great Doctor of Pain.

Idly, he traced blood across my chest.

"I have long wanted to torture this body of yours," he said. "It is perfect. You are unworthy of such perfection."

For most of my life I had been unable to comprehend my "Uncle" (for so I thought of him – how funny it was!), and once, when I'd newly learned about such things, I was certain he was one of those who lusted after young boys. Then I decided he merely lusted after pain.

But I did him wrong, truly, for Thulisquar was a pious and dutiful man, devoted equally to religion and science, to the twin paths of truth as he called them. He knew that the gods may only be reached through offerings, and that an offering devoid of impurity is like clear water. Through it we may see to the infinite bottom of the divine pool. In what he saw as my beauty, he discerned such clarity. I am sure that he sometimes wondered whether or not he had read the situation wrong on that day when he found me as a small child, starving near to death in the alley behind the Ministry of Pain.

Perhaps the gods meant me to be his victim, rather than his assistant and heir.

I was certain he was entertaining such doubts at that very moment.

"Get up," he said, prodding me with the whip. "Cover yourself and come along. We have important work to do."

I fumbled for the bedpost. He grabbed my wrist and hauled me up. I dropped down onto the floor with a thump, searching on hands and knees for my clothes. I had just struggled into loincloth and undertunic when he seemed to lose all patience. Snapping the whip, cursing under his breath, he seized me by the hair and hauled me out of the room. I desperately snatched up my remaining clothes. I wasn't sure I'd gotten both shoes.

Outside, I stood in knee-deep snow, the bundle of clothes in my arms. In the dim light, my legs and the snow seemed exactly the same color, the same substance. It was very funny. I imagined my flesh drifting away, the wind whispering through my bones, my toes snapping off like icicles and rattling down through the sewer gratings.

Thulisquar made me stand there for a few minutes, perfectly still. He stood behind me and held me firmly by both arms.

"The cold will sober you up," he said. "I need you to be at least slightly in command of your faculties. This night we have tasks to perform of unimaginable importance, and there is, I suspect, little time remaining to us."

(Suddenly, it wasn't as funny. I held the bundled clothes tight against my chest and throat.)

Thulisquar raised a hand, and the black, ornamented carriage of the Ministry of Pain lumbered out of the darkness, its matched black horses snorting white plumes of breath. He shoved me in, got in after me, closed the door, tapped on the ceiling, and we were off. I dressed as best as I could as I sat opposite him, trying to gauge the swaying, jolting motion of the carriage. More than once I slipped onto the floor.

"I cannot truly express how terribly, terribly disappointed in you I am," he said. "I feel my efforts with you have been a total failure."

I was ashamed then, and cold, and afraid. I managed to put on my trousers, overtunic, and vest. I'd lost coat, shoes, and socks entirely. I sat staring forlornly at my bare feet.

Soldiers stopped us at the gateway of the inner city. A sergeant scarcely older than myself leaned into the carriage. I watched his face, fascinated at the expression of extreme loathing as he recognized Thulisquar, then at the look of pity when our eyes met. Doubtless he took me for one more of the Doctor's victims. I noticed the red ribbon of the Revolutionary Party around the barrel of his musket. But things were still unsettled then. He dared not lay a hand on Thulisquar just yet. He let us pass.

* * *

And so we came to the familiar battlements, and the huge, round tower which comprised the Ministry of Pain and Revelation. There's a legend which says the tower is a great spear, rammed deep into the heart of the world, with only the very tip of the butt visible above the ground. The common folk say you can hear the moans of the Goddess Earth from that tower.

Most of the time we keep the doors and windows bolted, to contain the sound. (So very funny, once more.)

Down we went, into the earth, Thulisquar dragging me by the arm, around and around the circular stairs past one level, then another, where on the holiest of days, torturers descended in solemn procession on their way to celebrate the Mysteries, holding aloft the still dripping skins of criminals like banners.

No warders met us. Most of the staff had already fled, fearing the disturbances in the city.

So Thulisquar took the great metal key in his own hand and opened the final door to the Chamber of Revelation himself. As the cold draught from within blew over us like the sighing breath of a god, all sense of hilarity left me. This was a secret, truly holy place, where sometimes the gods revealed themselves in the utterances of dying men.

My Master turned to me once, and said, "I shall learn all the details of your juvenile excesses some other time – including, especially, where you got the *hanquil* – but now we have work to do."

Then we got to work as if nothing had happened. As I shuffled about with a taper, relighting lamps, I dared to hope that Thulisquar would become so caught up in his researches that he would actually forget my lapse.

Someone urinated on me from above, out of the darkness. I shoved my taper up through swinging iron bars. That which was burnt squealed like a monkey.

For all there was no one around to fetch us more subjects, I realized, we still had a healthy supply of experimental material – political criminals, condemned by the Satrap, sent here, and forgotten, since more immediate troubles occupied the ruler's mind these days.

It was here that my dour Master engaged in his own, private study of *hanquil*. As their bones were slowly crushed between massive wooden rollers, Thulisquar would lean over to listen to the last gasps of drugged men. And he could hear, *yes!* ethereal giggles which seemed to emanate from the Void. A wonder! Notations were kept in special ledgers, the data carefully correlated, its secrets laid bare for Thulisquar's meditative scrutiny by –

"*Oof! Wha– ? Excuse me. How did I...? What hour is it?*"

– a notary in attendance, over whom I had just stumbled, a bewigged, lanky, and malodorous *hanquil*-addict who lent his presence and stamp to each execution. Anthexis was his name. The Satrap had spoken to him frequently in former times, before affairs of state became too worrisome for such pleasantries. The wife of Anthexis stank too, but of perfume. She wore finery set with tiny mirrors that she might dazzle onlookers. She encouraged her children to spit at their servants. But Anthexis was merely an opportunist, a five-grain slave of the drug, neither philosophical nor vicious.

He staggered to his feet and helped me light the lamps. Above, the prisoners whimpered and cursed and prayed in their dangling cages.

(In truth I had obtained my own illicit supply of *hanquil* from none other than Anthexis. I wondered what the Master Doctor would do when he found out.)

One other staff member remained to us. I found him asleep on straw, the burly, black-masked Chief Torturer of the Jails. I knew he would not flee. This was his home, his entire world. He knew nothing else.

So devoted was he to the worship of the twin gods of Pain and Death, that he had long since given up his name and his humanity to them. So fallen was he from the known spectrum of human behaviors that he merely lay about when inactive, as a dog would, and could be identified and summoned by any barking noise. All curs, therefore, could hail him. This pleased him mightily in some way I never could quite fathom, and gave him a kind of mystical kinship with hounds and hyenas.

He was reputed to roam about cemeteries at night on all fours, tearing up fresh graves with teeth and clawed hands.

I barked. He leapt to his feet quickly, as a dog would. Above, the prisoners cried out in anticipation of fresh enormities, and the Chief Torturer fairly beamed with joy. The wails of the suffering and the innocent were

especially sweet to his ears, a kind of salve for his lesioned soul. For him
the bloody, sweat-soaked apparatuses of our work were like musical
instruments, human-stringed, and he, the Torturer, was a kind of virtuoso
attuned to the highest pitches of pain. Yes, in his own way he was
completely sincere, as totally devoted to his art and to the Twin Gods
whom we worship above all others as is any ascetic who spends his entire
life atop a pillar or walled up in a cell.

But I knew that Thulisquar found him revolting and merely useful. It
was an uneasy balance. Yet it would have to do, especially this night.

* * *

"I want you to watch and listen very carefully, my dear boy,"
Thulisquar said during a particularly protracted execution. (So I was a
"dear boy" now. Perhaps he *had* forgotten my offense. I tried not to
giggle.)

He signaled to the Chief Torturer. The rollers halted and I held the
funnel while Thulisquar ever so carefully dribbled a quarter grain of
liquefied *hanquil* into the criminal's mouth. Then he lowered his ear to a
mere inch above the lips of the expiring man.

The victim seemed to sigh, but Thulisquar trembled with excitement.
He, clearly, had heard more.

Then the sound came again, much louder than I had ever heard
before from anyone, a sharp, recoiling chuckle. It echoed and re-echoed
in the vast chamber. Above us, in the cages, the remaining subjects
screamed.

Thulisquar was ecstatic. He turned to me first.

"Did *you* hear it? Truly it was the god-laughter. Yes, it was! We are
close, so very close to our goal. Soon, by this means, mortal men shall
communicate directly with the divine. Think of it!"

"I am very glad for you, Master," I said softly.

That was not the response he had been expecting. His face clouded.
For an instant, I thought he would strike me. Then he turned to the
Notary Anthexis, who sat with pen in hand and his ledger in his lap.

"And *you* – "

Anthexis yawned. "I must have dozed off – "

Thulisquar let out a wordless snort of rage. He shook his fist at the
impassive Notary, but then his excitement overwhelmed all other emotions.
He turned to me again.

"Surely the god-laughter seems more pronounced than ever before."

My mind was still sluggish with *hanquil*. It took me almost a minute to recognize my cue, as if I had been an actor in a play. I fumbled for my line.

"Undoubtedly. Definitely."

Satisfied, he turned back to the Notary.

"I suppose so," said Anthexis. "But let us seek the confirmation of our burly friend here."

The Torturer's reaction was duly sought. No reply. Only a few grunts. The unanswered question hung heavily in the air. Then Thulisquar put this very question to the dying man entangled in our machinery.

The victim seemed to concentrate very hard. Thulisquar raised a finger. The rollers inched forward, over the man's pelvis. Blood spurted from his nose. I put the funnel down and gave him an injection of *madat*, a distilled *hanquil* derivative used to soften bones. It was his eighth this session. *Madat* extends a subject's survival considerably. His bones become like clay, rather than shards and powder. Sometimes we mold them into amusing shapes.

Thulisquar repeated his question.

"Nothing. I heard nothing," the dying man gasped at last.

Thulisquar paused, then said, "Do you suffer much?"

"Eh?"

Suddenly I didn't want to know. The after-effects of the *hanquil* now made me squeamish. I fidgeted with the injection needle I still held. The Chief Torturer looked up from the array of levers as he worked.

At last the captive spoke again. "It is a question without meaning."

"No suffering at all? Not the slightest discomfort?"

"None." The man wrinkled his brow as if deeply perplexed. Then he *laughed*, but it was only his own laughter. "It is getting harder to focus my thoughts, however."

Thulisquar turned sharply to Anthexis. "Write all that down. Subject declares himself insensible to pain." Then he snatched the quill from the Notary's hand. He tickled the dying man's forehead.

"Surely, fellow, you can feel this."

"Ah, surely. It draws me, a little bit, back into your world."

Thulisquar jabbed the man's cheek with the point of the quill.

"And you have no fear?"

"It is too complicated to explain – "

He turned again to Anthexis. "Are you getting all this – ?"

The Notary reached feebly for his quill. Realizing his error, Thulisquar gave it to him, and waited as the account was brought up to the moment in the dying man's blood.

A terrible smile marred the prisoner's features.

Thulisquar leaned over to me again. "Now watch closely, and understand. This wretch was an artisan once, a sculptor of statues. He will have the sensitivity to appreciate my own creative efforts, as one artist to another."

A small giggle escaped my lips. Perhaps it was the lingering *hanquil* fumes from the funnel I held.

"It was similar irreverence that brought him here," Thulisquar said sternly. "Something about a scurrilous caricature of one of the Satrap's wives. Have a care, Ganzeric."

Once more I was ashamed and afraid. I tried to be attentive.

Thulisquar turned back to the prisoner and bade the Torturer advance the rollers again, ever so slightly.

"Exactly what *are* you experiencing just now?"

"A...difficulty. It is so hard to exist...to...be. Squeezed. Broken. You have made an abstraction of me...a blot on the page."

At the Master's instruction, I once more placed the funnel in the man's mouth and we administered another quarter-grain of *hanquil.*

"Have you indeed *no* fear?" Thulisquar asked, bringing his face nearer and nearer to the criminal-sculptor's own.

"I am not...of your world anymore. I no longer care for anything you would understand. I am on the edge now, the very threshold...."

"*Yes?*"

"I...*nagnn* – "

It was at that exact instant the inspiration came to me. Perhaps I, too, was becoming caught up in the excitement of the quest. Perhaps the very gods moved through me, desiring to speak at last, instructing mankind as to the proper method of communication. Or it might have only been the *hanquil.* I could not be sure. But I forgot all else. I had to speak. "Master, if I may venture to suggest – "

Thulisquar jumped up, whirled around.

"Shut up, you imbecile!"

"But I see the answer now. If only you would – "

"You dare advise *me* – "

"...unmaker of men," the dying one said. "A reverse god...."

Thulisquar turned back to the experimental subject.

"Master," I tried to break in.

"Shut – "

He waved a hand, apparently confusing the Chief Torturer. Maybe the man was just clumsy.

With a clack and a rumble, the rollers broke free of all restraint, *consuming* the ex-sculptor. Brains splashed over Anthexis, who screamed and tumbled from his chair, then rose to his knees and desperately wiped the ledger clean with the corner of his robe.

"Idiots and imbeciles," Thulisquar ranted. "All I have to work with are idiots and imbeciles – "

"If I may only suggest – "

He grabbed me front of my tunic and yanked me entirely off the floor until my face was level with his. His eyes were filled with hate. I was certain he would kill me then, but, somehow, I was not afraid.

"What were you going to suggest?"

"The answer, Master. It is so clear."

"It is, is it?"

"Yes. It suddenly came to me. The *hanquil.* If you give a man six grains, he dies laughing. But if you give him *seven, very suddenly, before his body has time* to die, he is propelled beyond the threshold of life and death, into the other realm, where he can speak to the gods. *But he has several minutes left before he actually dies.* In that interval – "

The anger left my Master's face. He was stunned. He let go of me.

"That is actually a brilliant idea. Coming from you, it is a miracle."

I hoped then that he would actually forgive me for everything. But I dared not speak. The balance was *so* delicate.

"I must leave this place," he said at last. "I must walk and think. Come."

He started up the stairs, out of the chamber. I shuffled after him. He turned back to me.

"And Ganzeric – "

"Yes, Master?"

"Put some shoes on."

I had entirely forgotten that I was still barefoot. I glanced down and saw that my feet were black with the soot and dirt of the place. They were so numb with cold they seemed to belong to someone else. Therefore I had forgotten them. Such indifference is characteristic of the *hanquil*-user, I am told.

I borrowed a pair of boots and a coat from the Torturer. The boots were too big, so I stuffed them with straw.

* * *

So we walked together in the garden outside the Ministry of Pain. The common people dread it almost as much as the tower itself, but for me it has always been merely a familiar place.

Thulisquar paced among the frozen, crucified corpses, some of whom had been there for months. He seemed to ask questions of the blackened, shriveled faces. Sometimes he listened, as if receiving answers. I did not doubt it.

Then, too, he led me into that section of the garden where the trees are human beings, alive, perhaps immortal, but permanently rooted in the soil and shaped, hideously or fancifully, as the imaginations of generations of Torturers and Doctors had fashioned them. Here a woman was on all fours, hands and legs growing into the earth, her naked skin long since turned the color of old wood. Only her head moved, from side to side, endlessly. She was, of course, mad, and her howls had faded into a faint whistling between her teeth.

Thulisquar used her as a bench. He invited me to sit beside him, but I could not. I stood before him as he rehearsed his thoughts. Ours was a dialogue such as the philosophers might write, my role in it strictly that of a secondary character, restricted to stimulating and directing Thulisquar with my replies.

"The gods speak to men through suffering," he said. "For this reason there are wars and plagues and devastations. Through each grand event, the pattern of a divine thought is revealed."

"And the pain of everyday life," I said.

"Yes, even as a woman's labor and bleeding announce to her that the gods have given her a child. Even then."

"And it is through suffering alone that we may reply to the gods."

"Yes, that is so," said Thulisquar, "but the interesting part is this: we may communicate with the gods through the sufferings of others. The sufferer, the dying man especially, may convey occult knowledge back to the living as he totters on the threshold of life and death. Deathbed revelations are a commonplace. But when death may be *elaborated*, then considerably more information may be gained than otherwise. A devoted student might interview hundreds, even thousands of dying men, and thus carry on a lengthy dialogue with the world beyond this one."

"But the problem is to clarify their dying," I said.

"Only when the traveling soul may see the road before it *clearly*, yes, when the soul is far beyond the body, beyond the initial confusion and darkness, but the body is *still capable of speech*, only then may extended contact with the divine become possible."

"That is the purpose of our labors," I said.

"Yes. Otherwise you and I would be monsters, and our work obscene. It is immoral to cause pain without reason, Ganzeric. Never forget that, lest you become a monster."

*   *   *

The Master rose and walked, past a grove of human trees where hundreds of incredibly long, spindly arms grew from each body. Some predecessor of Thulisquar had created them long ago, with the aid of bone-softening *madat*. Stick-like limbs swayed in the night breeze. The tree-men seemed to be begging alms. Their cupped palms were filled with snow.

Then he took out a key and opened a gate. We went through and abruptly emerged into an alley I had not seen in a long time, but which I almost subliminally recognized. It was, in effect, my birthplace. Here Thulisquar had found me, starving.

We walked in silence. Beyond us, in the city, there were shouts and explosions. I was afraid then that the Revolution had begun. I didn't want to go on. But Thulisquar was not afraid. He emerged from the alley into a broad avenue, into a mass of people engaged, much to my surprise, not in riot but revelry.

It took my *hanquil*-fogged brain several minutes to recall that this was the Feast of Turning, when the winter stars have progressed more than half-way through the southern sky, and if you stay up until dawn, you can see the stars of summer rise just before the sun.

The gods were born on such a night as this. They rose from the cold mud of their mother's flesh, out of the Goddess Earth herself, and stood on the banks of the great World River, hand in hand, in silence, waiting for the sun, dreaming of mankind. The heterodox suggest that the gods were less than solemn on that occasion, and cavorted wildly and drunkenly on the world's first night, to keep the cold away. These heretics (my Master has dealt with many of them) further say that the gods all drank themselves into a stupor, that they lie yet in the world's mud, oblivious to mankind, and that the divine laughter we hear, on the threshold of death or in the holy man's trance, is no more than an echo of that first and archetypal orgy.

On the Feast of Turning one can almost believe it. On this night the streets were thick with shouting, singing, cavorting crowds. Men and women were having sexual congress in doorways, in snowbanks, on the very paving stones, oblivious to the cold and the spectators and traffic. Boys ran through the streets carrying bowls of burning powder which thundered and flashed and showered sparks. More than once I saw such a one catch fire, roll in the snow, and come up laughing.

I too laughed at many things. I felt the *hanquil* delirium returning. More than once Thulisquar had to drag me away as I tried to join in the festivities.

If anything, the Feast was more frantic than usual because of everyone's fear of the days to come, and, also, as the crowds gave vent to their anger over centuries of misrule.

Many of the gatherings were distinctly political. Three times I saw burning effigies of the Satrap that night, and twice those of my own Master. One of the latter was accompanied by a smaller effigy which might have represented myself.

"I do not care about such things," was all Thulisquar would say.

Fortunately we were not recognized. We walked because it focused my Master's thoughts.

"I return to the subject of laughter," he said. "Why do the gods laugh at us?"

"So that we too may laugh, and lighten our pain," I said, resorting to an answer from my earliest studies. "Laughter is infectious."

"And why do they give us the gift of pain?"

"To moderate our laughter."

"But if the pain could be *extended*, so then could the laughter, which is the very real speech of the gods. This is the use to which I shall put your very brilliant suggestion, my boy. Yes, you have made a definite contribution, and for once I am actually proud of you." He slammed his fist into his open hand. "Yes. I know what to do now. Yes. Back to work. Quickly."

He began to walk in rapid, long strides. I ran to catch up with him.

"Master, there is one thing which bothers me still."

"What is that?"

"Surely someone has taken seven grains of *hanquil* before, accidentally.

What happened?"

"Surely someone has, fumbling with a bottle during some delirious revel. Doubtless they babbled strangely before they died. But no scholar was present, no one who could appreciate what had happened. The event was wasted. Do not worry, Ganzeric. We are the first to study this phenomenon. We are pioneers."

*   *   *

At the mouth of the alley outside the garden, there was a tumult. Thulisquar forced his way through the crowd.

"What is this? What is this?"

He came upon the body of a girl child, who had been trampled and run over by a cart. The wheel-marks were quite evident in the snow, right across her middle. She might have been eight years old. Fish- and dog-masked revelers stood over her, gaping.

"Let me through," said Thulisquar. "I am a physician. Perhaps something can be done for the poor thing."

He knelt over her and produced a small vial of *hanquil*, which he forced between her lips. I counted the grains, one, two, three, four, five, six, *seven*. Ah, my Master, always the tireless seeker of knowledge. The crowd stirred when the sharp fumes revealed that it was indeed *hanquil*. They closed in. Thulisquar looked up. His outer robe fell open, revealing his embroidered inner garment, the uniform of the Ministry of Pain.

The people recognized us then. I let out a little yelp. I was sure we were dead.

But their look was one of *disgust*, as if an enormous turd had been thrown down before them. They didn't even hate us. It was as if they *knew* we would soon be dealt with, that our escape was already impossible.

But Thulisquar cared no more for the common people's feelings than he did for politics.

The crowd made signs to ward off evil and moved away.

Thulisquar held the child's corpse in his arms, swaying gently back and forth, whispering in the dead ear.

I tugged on his sleeve.

"Master. There's nothing we can do here. We'd better get back, where it's safe."

As if to deny me, the girl's mouth fell open, and there *was* a sound, like the whistling of a wind from deep within a cavern.

"You hear that?" said Thulisquar. "There are traces of the god-laughter even *after* the death of the body! This is a new development. It is of enormous significance."

And there was another sound, something even more enormous:

The corpse spoke. In a very distinct voice, not at all that of a little girl, it said, *"Seek me not, O Man; but I will seek you out, until the two of us are one."*

"Holiness!" Thulisquar cried. "Ineffable holiness! The unmaker of men speaks to me alone!" His voice was almost a scream of triumph.

That whole scene was the key to my Master's character. Then, truly, I knew him for a man who was god-mad, driven insane by the quest for the divine, filled with the spirit of unworldly mysteries, as crazed as the priests of distant Zhamiir who slowly flay themselves as a lifelong work of adoration. He was never a cruel man, or a lustful one, or power-hungry. For Thulisquar there were only the gods and the knowledge of the gods, which he, through his science, might reveal to men. In his own way he was himself holy, his quest beautiful, his motivations utterly unselfish.

Why the revelation came just then, in such a manner, I never did find out. Things happened quickly.

"Come!" He was up and running, carrying the girl's corpse. It was all I could do to keep up with him in my oversized, clumsy boots. We ran through the garden again, back into the tower and down into the holy chamber. There he laid the girl down on a table and left her, perhaps for future experimentation. As it happened, I never found out that either.

* * *

Again we labored in the Chamber of Revelations. I think several days and nights passed. Deep below, one never sees the sun anyway. My body told me that I was very weary, that my exhaustion and *hanquil* haze and hunger had all blended into a single miasma. I cannot recall what secrets Thulisquar revealed to me.

I know he used a new and revolutionary technique, whereby the bodies of the condemned were first softened, marinated in fluids for hours, given endless injections of *madat*, while Thulisquar spoke on and on in great excitement and agitation, telling how at last we would have specific messages from the gods rather than meaningless giggles, how all the things we had ever done were righteous, even pious, because *truth must be served.*

I think he mostly talked to fill the hours before the first subjects were ready. Sometimes he mixed chemicals in beakers and alembics. If he told me what they were for, such knowledge slipped from my exhausted brain like water through limp fingers.

Incredibly, the Chief Torturer had fled. Therefore I had to work the levers and turn the rollers as best I could. Only Anthexis remained with us, raving in another *hanquil* state, but somehow able to write in his ledger. I was clumsy with the machinery. Anthexis spilled ink and drooled on the page. But Thulisquar didn't seem to care.

At last the first victims were ready. We passed them through the rollers, then stretched them on racks so that, while they still drew breath, they were living kites, their every inch of surface consisting of outraged nerve tissue screaming in agony.

Yet with four grains of *hanquil* the pain was numbed. With five, these travesties shrieked out laughter. I too laughed. It all seemed, again, very funny as we daubed them with festive colors and glued sequins and ribbons and gaudy feathers all over them. Then we hauled a dozen of them up to the roof and flew them, indeed like kites, high in the air. Every evening they were reeled in and fed *hanquil*, a tiny fraction of a grain *more* than the fatal sixth dose, and each evening that fraction was a little bit larger.

Because they were no longer men, they did not die like men. They flew overhead for a week and came down, their sequins and ribbons smeared with blood.

I must have slept some of that time, merely fainting with exhaustion on a bench or on the stairs or on the roof. I don't think I ate anything. It was all a delirium, yes, like a *hanquil* dream or nightmare that would not end.

But Thulisquar did not sleep. He was in his finest hour, and tireless. It was the climax of his life.

* * *

Yet it was a horror too, and a terrifying disappointment, because now that the barriers between life and death were totally removed, now that direct communication with the gods had been established, the results were only a few strange, disordered words, and a great deal of laughter.

"Laughter," said Thulisquar wearily. "The gods laugh at our handiwork. But still there have been no more clear messages since the eve of the trampled child. We must press on."

And another time he said, "How elusive the gods are, in the end," and wept bitterly.

And, yet another, I saw from the rooftop of the Ministry of Pain that there were fires in many parts of the city. The Revolution had begun.

"Alas," said Thulisquar.

"Master," I said. "It's done. It's time for us to go."

Even then rebel soldiers were battering down the outer gate to the Ministry. Only Anthexis, of all people, was brave enough to oppose them. He fought fiercely for a time, shooting arrows down into the mob, pouring boiling oil, hurling stones. Meanwhile, Thulisquar struggled on with our increasingly tattered human kites. We had to use the same ones over and over. We had long since run out of prisoners.

After a while I looked down from the roof again and saw that Anthexis was gone.

As the crowd had discerned on the night of the festival, there was indeed no escape for us. Down we went, down into the depths of the ministry, barring and bolting door after door.

We had only a few hours left.

Thulisquar sat, exhausted at last, by the rollers of the torture-machine, contemplating the vast mechanism, weeping.

"After all this," he said. "After coming so close, I cannot live *or even die* having failed."

It was our philosophical dialogue all over again. Far above, the mob broke through one of the doors with a crash.

I watched in horrified fascination as my Master took out a vial of *hanquil* and put a grain on his tongue, then another.

"Do you ever think about the gods, Ganzeric?"

"Yes, but not profoundly."

"Sometimes I think you are wise to shrug them off, as they shrug us off."

"Perhaps, Master."

A third grain, a fourth. He was free from pain now. He could not feel his own exhaustion.

"Do you know what they do? The gods, I mean. Can you imagine their purpose?"

"I cannot."

"The gods make men," he explained, "in order to have something to laugh at."

And I was laughing then, exhaustion, starvation, and *hanquil* fumes working together. Once one has been exposed to *hanquil*, even the smallest amounts have that effect.

It seemed so very *funny*. Not sad. Not horrible. Funny. The laughter of the gods had shielded me from pain at the last. The merciful gods.

"Do you remember that sculptor we executed…whenever it was?"

"Yes, Great Thulisquar. I remember."

"He was like a god. He exercised godly prerogatives in stone, creating what shapes he wished, to be admired or laughed at as he chose. It was laughter which proved his undoing, I believe."

"Master, you have explained why the gods made men, but do men have any purpose of their own, save as objects for the gods to look upon?"

"Ah. Do the statues enjoy their own society, speaking a secret language, expressing secret loves and hates of stone? Is there a secret political system among them? Are some lords over the others, even as they are all equal in the eyes of mankind?"

He took a fifth grain of *hanquil*.

"Yes," he said. "It is quite possible."

A fifth grain and he *did not laugh*. Such a great and amazing man was Thulisquar.

The shouts of the invaders above us were louder now. I heard the continual boom-boom-boom and a battering ram assaulted another door.

Thulisquar took a sixth grain of *hanquil*.

"Master!"

He showed no sign of weakness. He was not ready to die just yet.

"I wanted to see the face of a god. I wanted to be with the gods. Only the gods are real, not men. We are illusions, the *hanquil*-phantoms of the divine orgy, nothing more. Is that not enough? Is that not a magnificent thing, to live in a world which is a delirium of the gods? Is it not wonderful?"

He lurched to his feet and staggered against a worktable. Bottles and jars crashed to the floor. He had a needle in his hands, one we had used to inject the prisoners. He could not steady it.

"You'll have to help me."

I steadied him, and gave him the injection of the softening agent, *madat*.

Then he lay down on the ramp before the rollers, opened the *hanquil* vial once more, and poured the entire contents down his throat, at least twenty grains.

"I shall be with the gods now," he said softly. He was, strangely, more coherent than he had been in days. "I want you to help me. This last experiment is a very difficult and delicate one. It is only fair that I should be the subject of it. Only I would be able to truly appreciate what I shall experience. Will you do this thing for me, dearest Ganzeric?"

"Yes," I said, alternately weeping and laughing. "I shall."

And delicately, lovingly, I pressed his body through the rollers like a printer turning out a rare and beautiful etching. He was paper-thin, stretched upon a wire frame, his features reduced to an abstraction, only his face recognizable, transformed as it was with holy ecstasy in addition to the mere distortion of flatness.

He spoke to me, in the secret language of the gods, and he told me many secrets, which amounted to one thing: laughter to ease pain, pain to moderate laughter. That is the balance of the universe. The Twin Gods who are greater than all the rest are not Death and Pain, as the theologians would have it, but Laughter and Pain. Even those two.

* * *

Inevitably, the revolutionaries broke in upon us. The door of the holiest chamber burst inward and there stood a mob of soldiers and citizens, swords and muskets lowered, awestruck in amazement. They were led by that same young sergeant who had leaned into the carriage.

He bore a head on a pike – Anthexis's – which he turned to right and to left as if it were a magic talisman and he were dispersing the evil from this lowest dungeon. Behind him, a grizzled captain carried two heads by the hair. One I recognized as that of the Chief Torturer. The other, intensely mutilated, might have been the Satrap.

They came down the stairs, into the room. I worked calmly, decorating my Master with ribbons and sequins. I hummed softly as I painted delicate patterns on the parchment of his skin, illuminating him as a final tribute to his greatness.

The sergeant stared. He tried to push me away, but I resisted, and resumed my work.

"Have you no fear?" he said.

"It is difficult to explain."

(Someone whispered that I was mad. Another said I was a demon in human form.)

I began to laugh. Then the great Thulisquar laughed too, for he was now the true and unimpeded conduit of the gods. The messages through him were utterly clear, without any distortion.

His laughter was like thunder. The whole tower shook with it. The mob and the soldiers turned and ran. Some of them fell to their knees. Some stumbled and were trampled.

Only the young sergeant stood his ground, for all he dropped Anthexis's head in his nervousness. It occurred to me that we looked very much alike, that we might be long-lost brothers. Suddenly I was very fond of him.

None of this mattered to Thulisquar.

"Have you no fear?" said the sergeant, not to me, but to my Master. Somehow this clever young man had figured out what and *whom* he was beholding.

"None whatever," said Thulisquar, quite clearly. "I hear now. I see. I shall soon be fulfilled."

I knew what I had to do then. I took a little knife and cut the strings which held the stretched form of the Great Doctor in place. He floated on the air. A breeze blew him into my face, and he whispered into my ears. I could smell his sweat and his blood and a trace of *hanquil*.

Gently, fascinated, the sergeant peeled Thulisquar off, then – to my astonishment – released him, watching him float on the air, whirling in the eddies and draughts of the chamber. Up he went, out the broken door, up, out of the tower while we two followed on the stairs.

Outside in the courtyard, the mob waited at a distance. The sergeant and I stood there for quite some time, watching Thulisquar drift upward into the bright morning sky, until he was just a speck against the sun and we could no longer make him out.

*   *   *

Now I write in my cell, because I fear I have little time left. I fear that the mob will demand my death, by torture most probably. They will give me to some crude butcher, whose ministrations will be…inartistic and without scientific validity.

How they howled at my trial. The judge and the soldiers shouted for silence again and again, but it was no use. The good sergeant testified. I think he tried to save me. I couldn't hear what he said. Nor could anyone else, I think.

But there *was* silence when I was called to repeat, at the very end, what Thulisquar had said to me as we parted, as his paper-thin self was wrapped around my face and he whispered in my ear.

"He told me that the gods are unknowable," I said. "That was his own, endless punishment, that after all he had been through, he still could not grasp the mystery. Therefore we should not hate him, but pity him."

It was a fine speech. But again the crowd screamed for my death. I was returned to my cell.

*   *   *

I pricked my left hand with the needle when I gave my Master the injection. The flesh has become soft. I pass the time carefully molding it between my fingers, until my hand is webbed. It disconcerts my jailers.

*   *   *

Later. There is one more thing, even as I write. *Thulisquar* is outside my window. I see him there, drifting in the evening shadows, flapping in the air like a banner. I reached out to him, but it was like grabbing mist.

I sit down again. It is no use. I write a few more lines. These.

He whispers to me. Is the secret for me alone, or for all mankind? I am not selfish. Here. Let me share it. These are the words of the Master Doctor Thulisquar in his transcended state:

I am the unmaker of men.

*   *   *

They are coming for me now. I hear boots on the stairs outside. My fate has surely been decided. I think I am going to die. I almost long for that, considering the alternative, which is that I should be declared insane and locked away in a cage for people to stare at, as if I were some exotic beast.

The world is not ready for the wisdom of Thulisquar. They do not understand.

I long for him, to be with him, like him.

I weep.

Hanquil. If only.

Seven grains would be enough for me.

The Magical Dilemma of Mondesir

N OW THE TROPICAL NIGHT calls out to Mondesir; to the Great and Magical Mondesir alone the secret voice of the island speaks. Perhaps the huge moth fluttering at the window is a messenger of the loa gods. Even inside the room, luminous faces of the dead drift in the darkness like burning paper masks.

It is a crucial time. Something as vast as life and death is nearly upon him. He can sense that very clearly.

The night manager stands oblivious beside him, his sweaty face gleaming by candlelight.

"I don't care *who* you think you are, Silbert," the man says. "You *must* perform. You must go on – "

The manager is a blind fool. *He* will never see the ghost-masks. His eyes are closed to things of the spirit. Mondesir draws himself upright, swirling his cape about himself with greatest dignity. To laugh in the face of a blind fool, *that* would be unworthy. Silence is the best response to such prattlings.

Even the insult of being called *Silbert* – the commonplace name of a commonplace man – rather than *Mondesir*, he allows to pass.

The only customer in the lounge of the Cavalier Plaza Hotel is a sleeping drunk, a *blanc*, a *touriste* who for some reason has not fled with all the others as the tiny nation of Saint Victorinus descends into its latest "emergency."

Street sounds filter in from outside: distant shouts, a motor roaring, gunfire.

The night manager tugs at Silbert's arm. "Get out there – !"

Silbert puts on his silk top hat, hardening his features deliberately as he takes sword-cane in hand, deliberately manifesting that *other* aspect of his true self which he sometimes, blasphemously, explains as his *petro* nature, his dark and terrible side, like that of a god.

"I am *Mondesir!*" He spits. "The greatest magician of them all! I require an audience worthy of me!" The dead faces flutter about his ears like moths, whispering their secrets.

Cecil, the night manager shrugs, nodding toward the dozing tourist. "Eh? An *Américain*. Perhaps he will give you a few dollars. You require that more, I think."

Silbert-who-is-Mondesir scowls, but says nothing more.

The night manager smiles, his face, too, hardened. "Get out there, or you don't work here anymore."

*   *   *

Let it begin then. Now is the advent of the great and magical Mondesir....
With a further flourish of his cape, Mondesir bows, removes his hat and gloves, then straightens himself so suddenly he seems to leap. The faces of the dead withdraw now, discreetly, into the farther shadows.

Illusions follow: fire from his hands and mouth, a beautiful lady in white, no more than two feet tall, drifting through the air; golden coins tinkling down from the ceiling, only to vanish as they touch the stage floor. A parade of flashy wonders.

Suddenly, two white birds flutter upward, out of Mondesir's clothing. This has always startled crowds in the past. Even under electric spot-lights – back when the capital had power, or before the last hotel employee capable of starting the gasoline generator in the basement deserted – Mondesir's rapier work with the sword-cane would be hard to follow. By candlelight, it is impossible. The doves seem to freeze in mid-air as he skewers them and holds them aloft on the blade, bowing to the sound while tape-recorded fanfare.

An impressive silence follows, broken only by the sound of the night manager flipping over the tape on the battery-operated player.

This setting is all so makeshift, unworthy of the great Mondesir. The elaborate sunken galleon motif of the room, with its sequined fish nets, giant conches of papier-mâché and glitter, murals of cavorting mermaids and drowning pirates under arcs of doubloons, seems merely tawdry.

But worst of all are the empty chairs. The chairs mock him, their emptiness a kind of laughter, the one thing the great and magical Mondesir cannot bear.

For Silbert, a full house might mean a month's groceries and rent; a few months of such "fat nights" would secure marriage to his beloved, beautiful, money-besotted Eulalie, who prays to American dollars and wears a wad of small-denomination bills in a *pacquet* around her neck.

Were she here tonight, Silbert realizes with unbearable certainty, she too would laugh at him.

At least the sole customer, having slept through most of the first act, does not laugh.

"Bravo...." The bleary-faced *blanc* claps his hands heavily from behind the virtual citadel of empty glasses and bottles on his table. "Great show. *Wunnerful....*"

Even this absurdly meager acknowledgment salves Mondesir's wounded pride. Just a little. The magician bows politely before the American's table. *"Monsieur* is very discerning."

If the *blanc* detects any irony, he does not respond to it.

"Those birds...are they really dead?"

"Extremely dead, *M'sieur.*" The Great Mondesir holds out the two impaled birds for the American's inspection. Blood stains the white feathers and runs down the needle-like blade. Mondesir waves the little corpses as if they are of trivial account and don't constitute his meals for the next couple of days. "Why does *M'sieur* take such interest in slain birds?"

The *blanc's* gaze locks with Mondesir's. For an instant, the white man doesn't seem drunk, but intensely, obsessively alert.

"Bring them back to life and I'll give you fifty dollars."

Silbert/Mondesir gapes in amazement. "Why, I – *Monsieur* is joking – "

The American waves a hand, knocking bottles onto the floor.

"Are you a real magician, or just another fake?"

Mondesir draws himself up beneath his cape, once more assuming the full dignity of a great sorcerer. Again he hardens his face, concealing all emotion behind a mask of terrifying impassivity. "For a fee," he says, "I can kill men who are many miles away, cause abortions at a glance, summon the wind, or, yes, bring the dead back to life...." He pauses, then continues, trying to gauge the *blanc's* intention. "For a suitable fee."

"All right." The *blanc's* wallet bulges with bank notes. He lays five American ten dollar bills on the tabletop as if dealing cards. "Bring them back, and these are yours."

The conjurer hesitates. *"Monsieur* insults me."

The American drops another hundred onto the tabletop.

"But, ah, certain preparations are required. *Monsieur* can have no idea of the rigors, the risks – "

Two more hundreds.

Silbert's heart is racing now, his mind filling with thoughts of Eulalie, who would never laugh at him again.

"*M'sieur* is a serious student of the occult if he makes such a generous offer."

With a broad sweep of his arm, the *blanc* clears the tabletop. Broken glass skitters across the floor. Weeping, he lays out another hundred and another, and another. "Shit, I don't care about any fucking birds – "

Mondesir pretends not to understand the English profanities.

"*Merde!*" the white man shouts, holding up a trembling handful of bills. "It's all *merde*, unless I can get what I want – "

Very courteously: "And what does *M'sieur* desire?"

"My wife has just died. Killed today, by a bomb in the marketplace. We were just buying souvenirs when…They tell me that miracles can be purchased in Saint Victorinus…Tell me now, and don't fucking lie – can you bring *her* back? Never mind the birds. Resurrect *her* and I'll give you fifty thousand American dollars."

"*Monsieur*, I appreciate and share your grief," the magician says, though Mondesir does not, any more than his other self, Silbert, does. It is all he could do not to whoop for joy. "I tell you only the truth now. Yes, it is within my power."

And from this moment on, he says to himself, *I am truly and forever the indescribably great Mondesir. I shall use no other name hereafter, ever.*

"…fine, fine," the American is saying. He scribbles down an address on the back of a business card and hands it to Mondesir, who knows the place, a fine funeral parlor for the rich, often patronized by the island's military rulers, their families, and their prominent and prominently assassinated opponents.

"I shall come at precisely midnight, and you will await my arrival," he tells the *blanc*, his voice now commanding, no longer polite. "For that is the hour of the mightiest sorcery, for which I must now make myself ready."

The American sweeps most of the bills back into his pocket, leaving only the original five tens for Mondesir. "A down-payment."

"My magic, *M'sieur*, has already begun its work. Therefore, be content."

The white man's eyes glisten with puzzlement and pain. Mondesir can see no hope there, much less contentment.

But what can a common *blanc* know of the abilities of the Magician Mondesir? Eh? Nothing.

* * *

Later, Cecil the night manager takes Mondesir forcibly aside.

"*Le Grand Boss* has a policy against mingling with the guests."

"The great Mondesir does not mingle. We were conducting business."

"What kind of business?"

"Fifty thousand American dollars."

The manager pulls his chin and sits down in a wicker chair.

"That's quite a lot for a lounge act. What does he expect you to do?"

Mondesir stands rigid, barely deigning to glance down at the other. "He has engaged my services in order to bring his wife back to life."

The night manager's eyes widen. "What? You are no *bokor!* You're no more than a mediocre stage magician."

For once Mondesir can not control his fury. He raises the sword-cane to club the manager, but the other man doesn't even flinch. Mondesir freezes, holding the cane aloft. "I, the great Mondesir, have heard the spirits talking to me all my life. I see enchantments in the air, all the time, all around us. That is all I need. Saint Victorinus has many *bokors*, but there is only one Mondesir! My magic is greater than any *bokor's!*"

The manager waves a quick sign with his hand to avert bad luck. "Don't be a fool, Silbert!"

"The money is very important to me just now. Eulalie will accept me after this. How grateful she will be that *I* take her as my wife!" It is Silbert speaking, but Mondesir finds his intended machinations useful.

"Money should not be a condition of love," the manager sighs.

"*Le Bon Dieu* has laid this opportunity at my feet. I must take it up."

"No. It is an evil thing you contemplate, Silbert. Such *diableries* please only one Personage."

Slowly, the Great and Magical Mondesir lowers his cane. It remains beneath his dignity to strike this ridiculous, brainless worm who can never hope to comprehend the ineffable wonder of Mondesir. He plunks his top hat on his head, takes sword-cane in white-gloved hand, and turns toward the door with his finest stage-whirl –

– only to be confronted by the imperious *Grand Boss*, owner of the

Cavalier Plaza Hotel, Emil Jourdemayne himself, who informs him there will be no second show tonight..."or any night. A curfew has been imposed. Saint Victorinus is under martial law."

"Go home, Silbert," the night manager whispers. "Just go to bed and sleep and forget about the crazy *Américain*."

"Silbert? *Silbert?* I do not know anyone by that name. You are the one who is crazy, *mon ami*."

Cape swirling with practiced nonchalance, the Magical Mondesir strides out into the night.

His magic has already begun its work, transforming Silbert into Mondesir for the last time.

* * *

Mondesir walks fearlessly through the streets and back alleys of Brinvillier, among the omnipresent soldiers who are more often than not gathered in clusters to club some unfortunate with their rifle butts.

He steps over a corpse with greatest dignity, ignoring groans and garbage smells from the darkness around him.

The air is thick with frenzied, frightened magic, the fears of hunted and dying men having assumed the shapes of bats, owls, and huge, flabby, featherless birds that scream with human voices.

And *only* Mondesir can see them. *Magicians have eyes of living crystal*, the saying goes. *Everyone else's eyes are mere water. Crystal sees what water cannot.*

On the outskirts of the capital a sneering lieutenant stops him, ordering him to do tricks, while enlisted men gather around.

The great Mondesir merely shrugs, preoccupied with far greater concerns.

Someone pokes him with a bayonet, observing the bulging pockets of his waistcoat.

He draws out the two dead doves, now neatly bagged in plastic so they won't stain his tuxedo.

"What is this?" the lieutenant demands fiercely. "Eh?"

Without a word, Mondesir begins to juggle the avian corpses with his left hand, but the headlights from a circle of jeeps dazzle him, ruining his timing. The doves burst from their bags, smearing his white linen shirt with blood as they bounce off his chest.

A gangly adolescent soldier with cream-colored skin flicks burning matches at Mondesir's tuxedo and cape, laughing.

"Now make yourself disappear, magic man!"

Scooping up the two dirt-encrusted doves, barely able to restrain his rage, Mondesir flees into the tropical forest that begins just footsteps beyond the city limits. Jungle darkness swallows him as suddenly as if he has plunged into the sea. As he gropes through the leafy underworld, he trembles, trying to regain his composure.

With a glance, with a simple invocation of the *Guédé* spirits, he could strike these soldiers dead. But they do not matter. Instead, he magnanimously forgives them.

He strolls on for perhaps half an hour, while the sounds of the city behind him give way to the less familiar night-sounds of the wild. A late, waning moon flickers through the breeze-tossed leaves.

Unlike many *blancs* or city people, or even *Silbert*, Mondesir has no fear of the birds in the branches, the wind in the trees, nor of serpents in the dark. The spirits hover in the trees now, everywhere around him. They will protect him.

Then, something else: the bleating of the ceremonial *lambi* horn which suggests a legion of red-shirts on the prowl. *Silbert* should be terrified of capture, of being dragged before the *Empereur* of the secret society to be condemned to some particularly grisly fate as an intruder, perhaps even subjected to the terrible death-powders that are the art of the *bête sereines*, the men who walk by night...ah, but *Mondesir* is quite above such childish devices as secret grips and passwords.

"I am not afraid of the living!" he shouts aloud, startling the night birds. "And I have urgent business with the dead! Fifty thousand dollars worth – hah!"

"You are a prideful fellow, Silbert – "

He turns sharply, baring the blade of his sword-cane.

"Who dares? Who dares address Mondesir thus?"

Something rustles in the bushes nearby. He thrusts the sword in that direction. The response is tittering laughter, from behind him. Another turn, thrust, more laughter.

"Very well then: Mondesir. You are still a prideful fellow. And a foolish one. Your friend who told you to go home and go to sleep and forget everything was the wise man, not you."

Mondesir gasps in amazement, then sighs, and smiles.

"Cecil, that must be you, having your little joke. You have followed me. The Magical Mondesir is not so easily deceived. Show yourself, confess your villainy, and I will find it in my heart to forgive you. If not, well...." Once more Mondesir's voice and visage assumes his hardened *petro* nature. "If not, well, who will account one more death during such a time of national emergency?" The sword-cane gleams by moonlight.

"*I am not Cecil.*"

Mondesir steps back in renewed astonishment as a robed thing no more than two feet tall emerges from a thicket, puffing into a conch shell, producing a low, bellowing noise that now does not sound at all like a laugh.

The thing's stature suggests a dwarf or a child, but its inhuman, side-to-side gait is more that of a gigantic crab. Mondesir can discern no face at all, though the tip of a bicorne hat juts out of the cowl. Bright red pantaloons of antique cut flash beneath the robe.

The thing fingers a wooden staff carved in the shape of a bird-headed serpent, its clearly visible hand either diseased or naturally scaled, like the hide of a crocodile.

"What are you?"

"That which Mondesir summoned."

"I didn't summon anyone."

"You did, in your mind. Surely the great magician Mondesir can summon with a mere half-formed thought. Surely he braves the dangerous jungle by night for the express purpose of meeting one such as myself."

Mondesir sheaths his sword and removes his top hat, bowing politely, if a little uncertainly, still unconvinced that this is any more than a joke to humiliate him.

"Of course I can. Yet I ask you again, *Monsieur*, to identify yourself."

"*I am the demon Biscornet.*" The creature's sepulchral voice belies its size.

Slowly, Mondesir puts his hat back on.

"Oh, very fine. You can work for me, if you will be honest and tell the truth. When the great Mondesir is impressed, that is something special. I will hire you as my assistant."

"I am one of the great lords of Hell. And I have come to assist you."

"Ah, St. Andre, St. Lazare – here I am ready to confront a *convoi* of red-shirted *Bizangos*, and this is what I encounter. A crazy, pantalooned dwarf claiming to be a demon!"

"Follow me." The creature turns its back and scurries through the underbrush. Cursing, heaving branches aside, Mondesir pursues until they reach a moonlit clearing. There, the supposed demon faces him, drawing back its hood to reveal a red beetle's face which, disquietingly, does not seem to be a mask, its plated insect jaws twitching continuously, drooling slime. "You, Mondesir," the thing says, "aspire to great deeds, to wonders and miracles, to, yes, raising the American woman from the dead in exchange for fifty thousand dollars."

Silbert, within Mondesir, is sick with terror. No jokester could know as much of his secrets, his thoughts, his desires.

And, something more: in the presence of this Biscornet, the forest spirits, even the bleating *lambi* of the red-shirts, are utterly silent.

"Furthermore," Biscornet continues, "you wish to accomplish these things *by yourself*, not as a *bokor* would, possessed by a god. Mondesir is no mere steed of the *loas*. He is a great sorcerer in his own right – "

"I wish," Silbert whispers, "to be destroyed – "

"Ah."

"– so that I may be born again by secret rite, to be entirely Mondesir the Great, with no trace of my former self remaining."

The demon's pig-like, cloven foot brushes *vévé* diagram in the dirt. "Perhaps this rite has already commenced, even as Mondesir suggests."

"What must Mondesir do?"

"Those birds; they are for me?"

He removes the two doves from of his pocket. "They are dead, Master."

"I like them that way. Death from life. Life from death. Do not call me master, for this night we are colleagues, Mondesir and Biscornet, partners and equals."

Mondesir bows politely once more, offering one of the birds. The demon snatches it faster than Mondesir's eye can follow, whether swallowing it or hiding it under its cloak, he is uncertain.

"Not everyone shows me such courtesies, Mondesir – me, one of the Great Lords of Hell."

"It is a fallen world, *Monsieur* Biscornet."

"So it is. Ah, but look where we have come to."

Mondesir glances up, startled, unaware they have come to any place at all. To his right, a path opens into the clearing. At the far end, clearly visible, stands a village, lighted by the occasional kerosene lamp.

The demon shuffles along the path, loudly thumping with its staff. Mondesir follows, astonished, but not totally surprised to find himself standing before the *la-cour* where his beloved Eulalie lives with her invalid grandfather.

Gran-père Theót snores away under a mango tree, cradling a nearly empty bottle of *clairin* in his lap. That is certainly no surprise.

What does seem completely incongruous is the undented, unrusted *camion* parked nearby – a fancy vehicle of unknown ownership, a fantastic intruder in this impoverished village.

Fear brushes lightly, then stabs, but Mondesir disdains fear as the quiverings of the soon-to-be-destroyed Silbert, who has long since ceased to matter.

"Look. There." The demon points with its staff and Mondesir peers into the shack through an open window. From within, laughter: Eulalie's soft giggle, then the throaty chuckle of another man.

The magician's eyes adjust to the renewed darkness. Staring through the bouquet of coral in the porcelain *jardiniere* in the window sill, Mondesir discerns two intertwined bodies: the delicate, caramel-colored form of Eulalie, and a hairy, grunting, fat creature on top of her – a *gros nèg*, a rich farmer that Silbert was introduced to several months ago at a *jook*-house dance.

Knees buckling, a rushing emptiness in his chest, Mondesir turns away struggling not to weep. Above all else, he must retain his dignity in the presence of the demon.

"Betrayal in love is a terrible thing," says Biscornet. "What will you do?"

"I don't know…." Mondesir squeezes his sword-cane so hard his knuckles are nearly white.

"*Silbert* is indecisive, but the wrath of the great *Mondesir* is certain and terrible."

"Yes, it is."

"Take this. Do what Mondesir must do."

He feels something pressed into his hand: the lantern which had been dangling from a nail by the door.

"What – ?"

"Surely I address Mondesir, not Silbert – "

In furious anger, Mondesir hurls the lantern in through the open window – not of the shack, but of the rich farmer's car. Spilt kerosene blazes merrily on the upholstery.

The demon's bows. "Very subtle are the ways of Mondesir. Let us withdraw to a safe distance and observe the terrible consequences of his revenge."

They step back into the bushes, watching the fire spread. Suddenly the automobile explodes in a thundering fireball like something one might see in a war movie on those rare occasions when the television set in the lounge of the Cavalier Plaza Hotel is actually working.

Gran-père Theót awakens, shouting a warning, but already too late. The blast has all but leveled the flimsy structure. The ruins burn fiercely, like dry kindling. The fat farmer squeals like the pig he is, but Mondesir must avert his eyes when Eulalie emerges, aflame from head to toe, waving her arms, eerily silent. She crumbles into a flickering heap while *Gran-père* Theót hobbles into the village for help, apparently without ever having noticed her.

"Mondesir, doubtless, feels no remorse over these things," says the demon Biscornet. "None. He knows that after Eulalie has slept under the waters for a time, he can summon her back, and that one recalled to life will be forever obedient. She cannot betray him again."

"Let the flames consume her then, even as she was consumed by her own lust," Mondesir intones, trying to sound utterly resolute. But inside, he feels only confusion, not remorse, nor even anger. *Go away, Silbert. The Great Mondesir has displaced you forever.*

He bows to the demon, offering the second of the two dead birds.

"No, no. The Magical Mondesir is too generous. Save the other for some future need. It will come."

All around, the air is devoid of spirit-voices, as if even ghosts are struck dumb by what has happened and what is to come.

*   *   *

Midnight approaching, the Great and Magical Mondesir re-enters the capital city, the demon Biscornet leading him by the hand in the manner of an over-eager child.

"What was the address?" says the demon.

"Here is the card."

The American's business card bursts into flame between Biscornet's stubby fingers. "I know the place."

"And I, too."

Perhaps both of them are now invisible to common eyes. No soldiers challenge them. No one cries out at the sight of Biscornet.

Before the funeral home they pause, regarding the sign slightly askew over the doorway and the soft glow of candlelight from within.

Inside, a man's weeping: the American.

"Ah," says Mondesir.

"But wait. First a warning. Remember that nothing quenches the spirit of the restless dead, Mondesir. Not even by burning a revenant to ashes, not even by boiling it in lye, can you kill someone who has already died. Do not raise up what you cannot put down."

"Why are you telling me this, Biscornet?"

"Perhaps as a reward for your courtesies. Then again, I might be attempting to beguile you with demonic candor, to damn you utterly by making everything clear, so that your choices are freely made."

"I require nothing from you, Biscornet. I, Mondesir am the source of my own miracles. The mysterious power emanates from *me*."

The demon lets go of his hand. "So it does. That is your tragedy."

Mondesir raises his sword-cane like a club.

"What are you talking about?"

"Were you merely Silbert, a fraud, you wouldn't get into such situations. But there is real magic in Mondesir."

"Of course."

"After all, not everyone can see demons. Fewer still would consider bludgeoning one."

Mondesir lowers his sword-cane. "Enough of this. Let us go in."

"You go in. Freely. Few enter Perdition with their eyes closed, Mondesir. I shall follow."

"It shall be the finest entrance of my career."

*　　*　　*

"God damn, you actually showed up," the *blanc* says.

"God damn," Mondesir replies, bowing politely, placing top hat and gloves on a polished wooden stand, leaning sword-cane against it. "What did *monsieur* expect?"

"That you'd run off with my fifty bucks."

"Such cynicism. I, Mondesir, would never contemplate such a thing."

He takes in his surroundings, the interior of the funeral home decorated in showy, vulgar style, with oversized gilt-framed mirrors, bowls of waxed fruit and plastic flowers on the tabletops, cheap plastic statues of Catholic saints in the corners, a huge bundle of dried palm fronds in a brass spittoon. Perfume thick as incense smothers the air.

The *blanc* sits before a closed coffin, containing, presumably, the shrapnel-shredded remains of his wife. The undertaker lingers silently to one side, hands folded in front of him, glum as a wax dummy.

We have come to Death's Bordello, muses Mondesir. He gestures to the undertaker, says in a whispery voice, "Leave us now."

The undertaker steps out of the room, closing the door behind him. The white man places a thick envelope on an empty chair beside him.

"For you. For your work...for your efforts on my behalf."

Mondesir leans over and takes the envelope, slipping it into the inner pocket of his jacket. The American almost protests, but the magician merely raises a hand.

"Do not fear. I will do what I have come to do. *I,* Mondesir, am truly able to raise the dead. *You* are privileged to watch. But say nothing and do not interfere, whatever you see."

"All right."

"Good!"

Mondesir claps his hands once, and all the candles in the room burn a deepening red; claps again and the fires burn blue, fainter still as shadows close in; a third time and the flames burn black, plunging the room into utter darkness. The American gasps.

Gently, Mondesir lifts the lid of the coffin. The corpse reeks of embalming fluid, and, more faintly but unmistakably, of gasoline. He whispers certain secret names and words, making signs with his hands in the air above the dead woman's face.

The door to the room creaks. Furious at the intrusion, Mondesir looks up.

The demon Biscornet enters, now luminous in scarlet, clerical robes, a bishop's miter on his misshapen head. Mondesir does not acknowledge him. The *blanc* apparently thinks himself still alone with Mondesir and the corpse, and does not react at all.

"You will need this," says Biscornet.

Mondesir receives a clay jar from the demon, unstoppers it, and taps a few grains of powder onto the dead woman's lips.

He listens now with his magician's ears and looks with his magician's eyes of living crystal, until he finds the place where the American lady's soul lies bewildered and restless at the bottom of a stream, among the other newly dead.

He calls to her. It only occurs to him then that he never learned her name.

Nevertheless, he summons her.

"You will need this too, to light her way," says Biscornet.

"I really will hire you as my assistant when this is over," says Mondesir, laughing. But even the great magician is astonished as the demon holds up a dove in his cupped hands, the same bird Mondesir slew earlier in the evening with his sword-cane. Now the bird glows like a paper lantern, burning within.

"You return your offering?" For an instant he feels undeniable fear, certain that this was a trap.

"No, I loan it briefly."

"Ah." He accepts the bird, relieved. As long as the demon acknowledges payment received, it remains bound to the magician's will. Therefore Mondesir is still master here. Biscornet serves him, like an altar boy at a solemn mass.

"Perhaps you thought to offer me the second dove now."

"Perhaps. Perhaps not. My greatest need for it may yet come."

They work in silence.

"Are you sure you know what you're doing?" Biscornet asks after a few minutes.

"Yes," replies Mondesir without another thought. *"Certainly."*

Mondesir labors, with mind and magic, repeating under his breath the words known only to the dead and to the spirits of the dead, the *Guédé;* conversing with Baron Samedi himself in dreadful secrecy. The dead bird flutters from his hands, hovering like a thing of luminous smoke, revealing for the first time the dead woman's seared face.

Then the apparition vanishes as if down a long, dark tunnel, shrinking to a pin-prick of light, gone.

Once more, the utter darkness.

"Now we wait," Mondesir announces.

The American shifts in his seat, but says nothing. Several minutes pass.

Mondesir fondles the fat envelope in his pocket. Alarmingly, for just an instant, he is touched by deepest sorrow. Tears stream down his face as he realizes that he had murdered his beloved Eulalie.

Be gone, weakling Silbert. Do not bother me ever again, he says silently. *I shall raise her up as I have raised this one. The Great Mondesir is fully equal to such a task. I cannot fail, nor is any error possible.*

"Ah," he says aloud.

The pin-prick of light has returned, waxing bright as a candle as the dead woman's soul journeys from its underwater repose.

The corpse stirs. The American stiffens and gasps. Biscornet, by

Mondesir's side, titters softly.

The glowing bird again hovers above the dead woman's face. She opens her eyes, exhales a foul breath, and says, "Mondesir, do you know who I am?"

Startled, he steps back from the coffin.

"Why, you are the wife of the rich *Américain* – "

"No, you fool. I am the one you were thinking of when you violated the sleep of the dead. *I am Eulalie.*"

* * *

Even the Great and Magical Mondesir can never quite follow what happens after that. It is all a jumble of terror and pain.

The dead woman screams, sits up in the coffin and bursts into flame. The demon Biscornet shrieks in demonic hilarity and leaps at his face, mouth gaping, many-toothed, like that of an enormous lamprey, repeating over and over the words *"The Great Mondesir is fully equal to such a task. He cannot fail, nor is any error possible."*

Mondesir stumbles against the coffin, wrestling with Biscornet as the corpse embraces him in fiery arms and he, too is screaming and the American, somewhere far away, shouts an unintelligible babble. The coffin crashes to the floor.

Then he is outside, and there, waiting for him amid a column of thick, black smoke, outlined in fire, is the expensive automobile of the rich, fat peasant who had been Eulalie's lover.

The burning dead man opens the car door politely, bowing as Biscornet and Eulalie bundle Mondesir into the back seat.

Mondesir writhes; the death-car roars through the streets; Eulalie's arms crush him, searing his flesh. She tries to kiss him with her lipless, blackened mouth, crooning her eternal love for him, how she will never, never leave his side.

The corpse-candle *gros nèg* drives relentlessly. Biscornet, on the back of the front seat, gleefully flaps turkey-claw hands together, clacking pig-feet. The demon has lost it's bishop's miter somewhere in the course of the struggle.

"Mondesir! Mondesir! Truly the great Mondesir has the power to raise the dead! How awesome! How wonderful! All praise to the magician Mondesir!"

"No! I'm a fraud! I am Silbert! Here! Take this!" He flings the envelope containing the money at the demon, who yanks out a handful of bills, which immediately burst into flame.

"This cannot be. Has not Mondesir proclaimed as much, that he alone of all men has only his *petro* nature, his dark and terrible side, that the merely human, which is Silbert, is banished from his soul forever? Surely the Great and Magical Mondesir would never lie. No, he is a man of honor, of pride, of vast and impenetrable dignity. Hah!"

Eulalie buries her face in Mondesir's chest, weeping scalding tears. Mondesir looks to the demon imploringly, but Biscornet merely shakes his head sadly.

"Was it not greatest wish of Silbert, who is no more, to be transformed utterly into Mondesir, a magician with the power to raise the dead of his own accord, without the aid of the *loas?* So why isn't Mondesir happy? He has everything he wants. Even the loyal Eulalie has returned to him."

"No! I am Silbert! There is no Mondesir! He's just a stage name – !"

Suddenly the back door of the speeding car swings open. Eulalie lets go. The demon's cloven pig-feet are branding irons jammed into Silbert's buttocks just before he hurtles head-first into space.

"You are such a disappointment after all," Biscornet sighs.

* * *

Silbert awakens at mid-day, amazed to be alive, lying face-down in mud and sewage behind a ramshackle hut. A pig nuzzles him.

He rolls over and sits up painfully, shooing the pig away. Only flies buzz around his ears. No ghost-masks anymore.

He is nearly naked, his fine clothes smoldering tatters. The fifty thousand dollars, of course, has vanished. But something bulges in the remains of his vest pocket.

Both doves. Twin spots of red mar the identical, perfectly white breasts.

He sits there, uncomprehending, turning the bird over and over in his hands.

The demon did not accept payment, not that the end. No final bargain was ever consummated.

* * *

Much later, still clutching the doves, he staggers into an old cemetery and stands at the edge of a pit centuries old, where lie the bones of slaughtered Arawaks, the original inhabitants of the island.

"What a fine army you would make," he murmurs. "I could rule Saint Victorinus with my legion of the dead. No need for guns. No need for tanks...I could...if I were truly magical. But...Silbert is an arrogant fraud." He falls to his knees and covers his face with his hands, weeping, pressing a dead bird against either cheek. Blood runs down his neck.

Someone tugs gently at his arm.

"No, you *are* magical. That is your tragedy."

He screams and scrambles away, crawling backward, certain that he has confronted the demon Biscornet once more.

But the small figure before him is only a swollen-bellied little boy, naked but for a pointed, paper hat.

Silbert feels a brief instant of relief; then his helpless terror returns as he understands that some spirit speaks through this child.

"Eulalie shall return to her beloved each night, evermore faithful. No one can doubt the Great and Magical Mondesir after this."

Then the spirit leaves the child, who awakens startled, as if from sleepwalking, and runs off through the underbrush.

"It's all lies! I don't have any magic powers!"

He hurls both dead birds after the fleeing child. In mid-air they come to life and fly away.

The Paloverde Lodge

I THINK I CAN RECALL THE EXACT MOMENT when things were hopeless between Janice and myself, when there could only be pretense and sham in the future, but never true reconciliation. The moment came when the words "sexual martyrdom" occurred to me, as Janice lay naked beneath me on the sandy cliff-edge, in the buff on the bluff, so to speak, in the windy evening air which was cooling almost as rapidly as my ardor. She panted. She arched her back, clawing the ground and my back with her hands, putting up a good show, but she clearly wasn't enjoying herself. Her eyes were shut, her face turned away so I couldn't kiss her grimacing mouth.

And I thought then that she looked like Joan of Arc at the stake, waiting for the flames –

Right there. At that precise instant.

"Oh shit," I said, rolling off her. "This isn't going to work."

She lay still for an instant as if puzzled, then sat up suddenly, slapping her thigh.

"Ow! Something bit me."

Something bit me too.

"Jesus – "

"Let's get out of here," she said.

We started to dress and gather up our things. I could only reflect on how foolish we had both been, thinking we could abandon ourselves to ecstatic love in the Arizona wastelands when both of us were city kids, fretful about being away from telephones, libraries, hospitals, junk-food restaurants.

It had been her idea, as a last-ditch, crazy attempt to repair our three-year-old and rapidly failing marriage, to pull out of the fatal dive before the final, shrieking tailspin. We had hiked for three days, quiet much of the time, overwhelmed by the desolate magnificence of the landscape, by the awesomely dark, starry skies, and by, I think, the kind of ridiculous hope that flourishes as long as no one opens his or her mouth and begins to talk sense.

In the sleep of reason, optimism.

But something bit me on the ass and I woke up.

"I'm just tired," Janice said.

"It was your fantasy, remember?" I said, shaking my boots out for scorpions.

She muttered something, maybe not even words.

"It *was* your idea. Christ, there was a survey once, in which ninety-fucking-percent of high school kids said that if the world was to end in half an hour, they'd like to spent their last thirty minutes screwing on the beach."

"Like in that movie, *From Here to Absurdity* – "

"Or was it *To Heave and Heave Not?*"

"Shut up and come on," she said, shouldering her backpack.

The desert sky darkened, overcast and starless. A harsh, gritty wind blew, like God the Cigar-Smoker exhaling as hard as he could, and I had to hold up both hands to keep the sand out of my eyes. Nearly blinded, I tumbled into Janice, and the two of us fell into a cursing heap. Then, just as suddenly, the wind stopped and it began to rain. Within seconds were sitting with our butts sunk in mud.

"Just my luck," I said. "Nothing, but nothing seems to have gone right on this trip."

"Enjoy your second honeymoon, Samuel," Janice said icily. "It's the last one you're going to get..."

It had been a mistake, everything, not just the camping in the desert. Communing with nature, reading to one another from *The Teachings of Don Juan* by the light of an L.L. Bean Sportsman's Lantern, nothing had worked out, nothing made us any happier.

I reached for her hand. She jerked it away.

"We gonna sit here all night?" she said.

"I guess not, dear," I said, rising, helping her to her feet. She accepted my hand that time, when the gesture was utilitarian, not one of affection.

"Shit," she said.

Neither of us said another word for nearly an hour as we slogged down the mountainside, utterly soaked, sliding in the mud again and again as the trail slipped away beneath our feet like lumpy pudding. She pouted all the way. Whenever lightning revealed her face, she was puffy-cheeked, her lower lip protruding, like a small child who hadn't gotten her way.

Finally I spoke up. "The rain will wash away our cares. Remember?"

"Shit!"

Somehow it never occurred to either of us to stop and make camp. We would be dry inside the tent, if our luck held – no, if our luck *changed*, for the better – but I don't think either of us wanted to be that close to the other. Walking, we could at least have the sensation of *leaving*. Exit from marriage, stage left.

Here we were, two high-verbal types, both graduate students in linguistics, reduced to gestures, to the physical act of walking when words and thoughts failed. Sure, I could appreciate the hilarious irony of it.

Sure.

* * *

It seemed like hours passed as the rain poured down, and more than once I considered the very real danger of being swept away in a flash flood. We slogged on, ankle-deep in mud, heads bent down against the wind, water pouring down our collars as a result, sagebrush and cactus scraping against pants legs as we blundered onward.

I tried to find something to be cheerful about, anything.

"Shit," Janice shouted. She made a march out of it: "Shit! Shit! Shit-shit-shit!"

"Eat your beans, they're good for your heart, the more you eat the more you – "

She whirled around and gave me the most poisonous look imaginable.

"You just shut up. Okay? Shut up."

"Look! A light! We're saved!"

For a moment I didn't think she believed me. She was about to hit me. But then she turned back and saw that there was indeed a light. Both of us ran for it. Lightning flashed again, and I made out sheets of water rippling across a road and a series of low, wooden buildings, one of them with a porch and a light in the window. A neon sign flickered by the edge of the road.

"Paloverde Lodge!" Janice gasped, slowing to a staggering walk. "Thank God."

"Any port in a storm."

She actually smiled at me then. "Damn right."

When we stood on the porch and knocked frantically at the door, thunder crashed again and again. Janice was shouting something. I couldn't make it out. But then the storm quieted a little, and I knocked once more and heard footsteps within.

"Let me guess," she said. "This place is owned by a ninety-year-old boozed-up desert rat named Pappy who hasn't seen a soul in twenty years except for his mule Esmerelda – "

That was more like the Janice I'd once known, who knew when to be silly. I slid my hand gently around the back of her neck.

"No, it's run by this very nice, but *strange* young man who never goes out much, but is very good to his mother. He has a *thing* about showers – "

She brushed my arm away.

"That's not very funny. You never were."

Before I could make any reply, the door opened, and the two of us sloshed inside. The air-conditioned air made us shiver. Our host was a silver-haired older man in a dinner jacket, who had been sitting at a table by himself playing cards. The room was a combination motel office and restaurant. There were three tables, a dozen chairs, and a juke-box in the corner.

"Greetings," he said. "Greetings. Have a seat. No, better yet, a towel. The laundry room is right up the hall. I'll be back in a jiffy – "

"That would be magnificent," I said, as Janice and I slumped into chairs.

"Help yourself to some coffee," the old man said, indicating a pot and a state-of-the-art coffee maker.

As soon as he was gone, I whispered to Janice, "So, what exactly do you propose we do?"

"Take a cabin. What else? I'm not going back out in that rain."

"And then – ?"

Before she could reply the owner returned, his arms full of big pink towels with bleach marks. The old man was beaming, his right hand out-stretched. "Didn't introduce myself," he said eagerly. "Jack McMasters's the name. Owned the Paloverde since I can't remember when. I've tried to keep the place from falling apart." Then his smile faded. He put the towels down on the tabletop between us and indicated the room. "It's so filthy. I have to apologize for that. I try and try and – "

I'd buried my face in a towel, but when I looked up and started to examine the room, I was genuinely puzzled. The place was spotless. The furniture needed a new coat of finish, most of it, the tables and chairs seemingly worn away by obsessive cleaning.

"You seem to be doing a fine job to me," I said.

He said nothing. I hoped I hadn't somehow offended.

Lightning struck very close. The panes in the windows shook. Seeing what he took to be Janice's alarm, the old man went on. "Don't worry about the weather. It's not like we're going to slide into the canyon." There was another pause. We sat listening to the rain. Janice glared at me, as if trying to flash a telepathic message of, *So, say something, stupid!* But McMasters ignored us and continued talking, almost as if he wasn't aware of us. It was a monologue, addressed to empty air, or, perhaps to someone else, out there, in the storm, someone listening.

I wondered who was going stir-crazy faster, me or Jack McMasters.

"Glad to have some real company for a change," he said, smiling. He sat down at the table with us, cutting the deck of cards, then offering them to us. "You play?"

"Not really…"

Janice kicked me under the table.

"A little," she said. "Well enough."

"Great." He dealt out three hands of poker. No one suggested betting anything. We played. I realized then that Janice and I were still sopping wet. Somehow we'd overlooked that small point in the confusion of the moment.

She sneezed. Then McMasters rose from the table and brought us both coffee, which we drank gratefully.

"Sorry," he said. "I forget my manners sometimes. Gets so a man forgets what it's like to be with his own kind – people, I mean." He laughed and made an ambiguous gesture. "What I mean is, we don't get much clientele this time of year – or any other, for that matter."

"We –?" Janice said.

"Only me. Only myself here." The old man poked his own chest. "Only the three of us." He seemed to be having difficulty saying something more. Then at last he managed, "My Loretta passed away not too long ago."

"I'm sorry," I said. That's what you always say. *I'm sorry.* The useless formula that heals no wounds. "Must get lonely here."

"Mister," Jack McMasters said intently, pointing at me across the table, "no matter what you hear about the pleasures of solitude, don't ever believe it. People are what life's all about. Living, breathing people. And love. And being young. There's still hope then. If anything isn't right in your life, there's still a chance you can change it. It isn't too late. The possibilities aren't used up yet." He gazed out the window, into the storm. "I envy you both," he said softly.

I reached under the table for Janice's hand, and she didn't resist me. I tried to gauge the old man's emotions, but couldn't. I think he suppressed a grimace, as if he'd felt a sharp stab of pain. Then he rose and fetched more coffee. He came back with a tray of donuts.

"On the house. As many as you want."

Janice and I each took one gingerly. Mine was stale. I didn't say anything.

"How long are you planning to stay?" McMasters asked.

"Not long," I said. "We'll have to be going soon." If then occurred to me that one doesn't carry much money on a camping trip, and quite possibly I didn't have enough on me to pay for even one night's room.

"You can't be planning to take your lovely wife out into that mess." He indicated the storm.

"Actually, we're lost," said Janice. "We'll be happy to stay."

I quickly pulled out my wallet and pointed, hoping that she'd see and McMasters wouldn't.

"Off-season rates, discounted at that," the old man said. He got up again and went to the window, gazing out into the night. Lightning flashed, illuminating his face. "Hell, you can stay for free – "

"We wouldn't want to take advantage – "

"Sam," Janice whispered. "How thick can you be. He's telling us he wants some *company* – "

"Look at this," the owner of the Paloverde lodge said suddenly, turning around. He drew a whole wad of bills out of his jacket pocket. "There's plenty more where that came from. So I don't need your money, believe me. You look like good people, clean-cut, with decent lives filled with hope and...*possibilities*. So, please, stay with Jack McMasters. On the house. Now tell me, what do you folks do with yourselves when you're not getting lost in the desert?"

I explained briefly that we were both graduate students, Janice a Ph.D. candidate, me closing fast on an M.A.

"Scholars, then? Loretta was sort of a scholar. Well, she didn't actually have a degree or anything. Never went to college. But she read books. She was real interested in the local lore. Indian stuff. It was in her blood."

"Oh..." I suppressed the urge to say more, feeling like an astronomer confronted with, *Oh, my wife was a space scientist too. She rode flying saucers all the time.*

"My Loretta was part Hopi. Had some Mexican blood too. She'd go away for days at a time, into the desert, searching for lost Indian burial grounds and such. There's one she found nearby. Bunch of stone markers arranged in some kind of pattern. That's where she...that's where Loretta rests."

Just then I heard a noise like a tree branch brushing against the window pane. Only there were no trees outside, I suddenly remembered. I looked up and saw someone outlined against the glass by lightning, a bent figure, ashen, emaciated.

Janice stifled a scream. "That man looks like he's been hit by lightning – burnt."

"Oh," our host laughed nervously. "Ignore that shabby bag of bones. Just a vagrant."

"How terrible," I said, wondering why I said those words, unsure of how a vagrant can be *terrible*, but certain somehow that I actually meant precisely that.

"Be back in a minute, folks." McMasters put on a hat and raincoat and hurried outside. For an instant the storm was inside the room, a blast of spray. Then the door slammed shut and the air was still. In the darkness, the ragged figure tapped at the window insistently. Janice looked at it, then away. I thought she was going to faint. I tried to convince myself it was just fatigue catching up with her.

Then Jack McMasters was shouting something over the roar of the storm. I got up and peered out. He had confronted the creature in the driveway, wagging his finger, pointing, repeating some word I couldn't make out over and over. The vagrant or whatever it was cringed, a sodden mass, almost shapeless. For a minute I thought it was a bundle of sticks and mud somehow come to life, not a person at all. But, no, it moved like a person, crawling behind a dumpster. Jack McMasters threw a rock after it, then another, hard, as if he were afraid or angry enough to do deliberate injury.

But then he walked over to the window, tapped in front of my face and smiled. Problem solved. He came back inside, dripping. For a minute or so he tried to continue the conversation, making some remark about how hard it must be to get an educational loan these days. I found myself mumbling some nonsense about grants and austerities. Then the old man noticed that *he* was wet to the skin despite his raincoat, and he suddenly produced a key, which I accepted without any argument. Janice was in no mood or condition to discuss things further.

"The Honeymoon Suite," Jack McMasters said. "I expect you'll want to get on dry clothes and rest up some. Then, dinner at eight. Only chili and refried beans, I'm afraid, though."

"That will be fine," I said. "Thanks."

I maneuvered Janice out of the restaurant. Her eyes were closed and her hands covered her face. For an instant the weather blasted us, but the walkway to our room was covered by a sloping roof, which helped a little. I glanced over toward the dumpster, wondering what had become of the vagrant, not really feeling sorry for him. I was beyond caring. It had been, all told, a ghastly day. Not uninteresting, but ghastly.

The Honeymoon Suite. Yeah, right. Stick the knife in. Twist.

* * *

Later, I watched the shadows of my wife as she washed in the bathroom. Against the dust-colored walls her shadow was black, evocative of Plutonic glooms. A thunderclap and a brilliant flash merely interrupted my contemplations. They resumed. The shadow put on shadow panties.

"Honey? Are you feeling a little better?"

"I'm a little dizzy. I hope it wasn't the donuts."

"Well, I was just thinking. We're in the Honeymoon Suite and, you know, I just thought – " I dared to hope, just a little bit. That's what I was really thinking.

"Forget it!" She emerged from the bathroom, bra-less, but pale and annoyed and somehow not at all alluring. "I just don't feel like making love after…that poor creature."

"It happens everywhere Janice. You can't help 'em. Neither can I. Even out here where there are no streets – street people. When it rains, they get wet."

"This one looked dead."

I glanced at my watch. "It's five minutes to our exotic meal at the exotic Paloverde Lodge. We mustn't keep the chef waiting – "

"Don't be a smart ass. He's being very good to us."

I watched her dress. Her movements were clumsy, tormentingly slow.

Twenty minutes had crawled by before we made our entrance, in our best hiking clothes, clean and only slightly rain-splattered. Jack McMasters was waiting for us, showing no sign of impatience. He wore a tuxedo of raw silk, blue and shiny, hopelessly out of date. I refrained from making any comment.

"While you were preparing yourselves," he said, "I went to Loretta's room and got some of her books. You two, being scholars and all, might like to have them."

"Thank you very much," Janice said.

He handed over three thick volumes, all from the later 19th century, all dealing with American Indian folkways.

"They look like more your field than mine," I said to Janice. Indeed, the tribal languages of the Southwest were her specialty.

"Thank you again," she said, putting them aside on the table.

Something rapped at the window. I looked up, more alarmed than I could account for, but there was only the glow of the neon sign; other than that, only darkness and rain. Cheerfully, Jack McMasters excused himself and shut all the drapes. Still smiling, he locked the front door. "The lodge is just not open for business tonight," he said. He flicked a switch and the neon sign went out. A second switch extinguished the porch light. "Now we can get to know each other better."

"These look like great books," Janice said.

"Loretta always said that books only go so far. Real knowledge, she always told me, couldn't be found in books."

I met Janice's gaze. She smiled unconvincingly and said, "Of course that depends on how you define 'real knowledge.'"

"I mean real knowledge of how the world works. The rules of life and death, as a case in point. Loretta insisted that 'real knowledge' is deliberately left out of books, that nobody could write it even if they wanted to, like it had a way of protecting itself somehow. Sometimes she's very opinionated, my Loretta."

Janice paled. "Sometimes –?"

"I mean she *used* to be opinionated. When she was still alive."

I felt a touch of real pity for the man. His dead wife still filled his days and his thoughts, as if she had never gone, because there was no one else for him.

"It must be very lonely out here all alone," I said, feeling slightly embarrassed, hoping he wouldn't take that as patronizing.

"Being alone is bad, like I said before. But there's worse. A lot worse. Nothing, I think, is lonelier than a bad marriage, one you can't get out of. An endless marriage...."

"These days there are always quickie divorces," Janice said, puzzled.

The old man scowled. "That's fine when two people want to go their

110

separate ways. But what do you do if the other person won't *leave?* What's a man to do if his ex keeps coming back, clinging to him, and not playing by the rules?"

I couldn't find anything to say, nor could Janice. We sat once more in awkward silence.

The rain. The wind. Thunder. Tapping at the window.

Sighing, the old man rose and began to serve dinner. "Rules," he said. "Like Loretta said, the rules that matter aren't in any books. You have to, I suppose, learn them some other way."

We ate in silence. It was not my idea of a pleasant evening. I did notice Janice glancing at the books from time to time, as if they were treasures she couldn't wait to dig into. I was glad for her. At least someone had gotten some benefit out of the fiasco our alleged Second Honeymoon had become.

The tapping at the window became louder, more insistent as, at last, the storm began to die down. I couldn't stand it. I wanted to shout something, even to run outside and confront the vagrant, whatever –

But Jack McMasters simply rose from the table and said, "Say, folks. There's something I have to attend to. Excuse me. I may be a while, so just leave the dishes on the table when you're done." He peeked out behind a drape, the put on his hat and raincoat, but left by the back way, through the laundry room behind the office.

*   *   *

Much later Janice and I managed to make love in the darkness of the Honeymoon Suite, not particularly well, but as long as we groped for one another wordlessly we did not argue and the function was performed. They we lay still for a while, listening to the silence of the distant wilderness, and the nearby dripping of rainwater off the roof after the rain had stopped. I must have slept for a while because I awoke with an aching stomach as the Mexican food refused to rest easy.

But I paused on my way to the bathroom. The window was open. Moonlight shone through, and in it, naked on top of the covers, Janice *glowed.* She was breathtakingly beautiful just then. It was all I could do not to weep, not at the sight of her, but at the realization that we *could* still turn back upon the path we'd walked the last few years. We could still love each other again, as we had, if we tried, for a while at least. As Jack McMasters had said, the possibilities weren't all used up yet. If only we dared –

As I returned from the bathroom, a cloud had covered the moon and the room was dark. A grunting noise from outside caught my attention. I went to the window and looked out.

The night was dark, but I could see clearly enough. I saw them outlined against the pale desert sand: the old man, half naked, and the other. I heard him sobbing in despair, and I knew the voice and I knew the man. It was Jack McMasters, bare-chested, arm-in-arm with the ashen creature. The sodden mass of its head rested on his shoulder, cradled against his scrawny neck. Affectionate nuzzling. Only then was I absolutely certain that the "vagrant's" contours were feminine. There was no mistaking it.

Ten minutes later I was dragging my half-dressed and still protesting wife down a muddy hill, both of our backpacks in hand, stumbling against stones and cacti. She kicked me once or twice. She screamed every obscenity she knew. I was stronger than her. I prevailed. After a while she went along quietly.

But I could not explain. I would not. Ever. I merely knew that there are far, far worse marriages than ours.

*   *   *

Janice and I were divorced when we got back to civilization. It seemed, then, the only decent alternative. As the years passed and we met again professionally, at conferences and the like, I found that I respected her more at a distance than I had when we were married. I even grew to like her.

But I never told her what I saw that night, and she never told me what she must have surmised. We do not share such intimacies. We have gone our own separate ways.

Those of the Air

DECLINE, DECAY, THE STENCH OF YEARS closed over me as I drove through Haverbrook Park that colorless wintry afternoon. My old neighborhood had become a hollow place of blackened brick and faded gray clapboard, peopled by phantoms from my past, by vanished friends, by deceased neighbors, by the aging effigies of my parents in their final, precipitous plunge into decrepitude – by everything I thought I had broken free of, the dust I thought I'd stirred for the last time, the chains I thought I'd cast off one evening, ten years before, when I'd screamed "Fuck this goddamn shit!" at the top of my lungs for no immediately apparent reason, packed a hasty bag, and stalked out of the house, informing my startled and but perhaps not entirely sorrowful parents that I wasn't coming back, ever.

I'd made that promise stick for ten years. Now I was coming back, one more time.

Because of an inescapable loose end. Because of Jeffrey, my half-mythic older brother, who wasn't able to leave as I had.

I glanced at the passing scenery: heaps of rubbish on sidewalks, a burned-out building that might have been a private home or a warehouse, but I couldn't remember which; four more stores closed, one of them Kohler's delicatessen where, thirty years ago, my father, then a young parent trying to show off to impress his embarrassed sons, used to pound counters and bellow for corned beef.

Now he wasn't much up to pounding or bellowing for anything, I knew, even before I pulled into the familiar side-street and inched my way behind the brick row houses, weaving among trash cans and the occasional tricycle until I came to our own, familiar, unpainted garage door.

He met me at the back door, after ten years no more than a wizened caricature of his younger self.

"Hello, Dad."

"Hello, Son."

I'm sure what he meant to say was more on the order of: *Why the Hell did you come back after all this time? I'd hoped you wouldn't have to.*

And I wanted to reply: *You know perfectly well. It isn't my fault, Dad. Or even yours.*

But so many of the important things never manage to get said. *Jeffrey is my brother. I can't help that, but he is.*

So, overnight bag in hand, I followed him slowly through the tangle of our basement, then upstairs, through the kitchen – a disaster area, far, far messier than I had ever seen it in my life – and into the still immaculate, plastic-covered living room.

He sat on the plastic-covered sofa, too weary to continue, his very presence a stain on this inviolate shrine of a room.

I remained standing. I tried not to touch anything. An awkward silence followed.

Finally, Father ran a liver-spotted hand over his almost bald head. He sighed.

"You look different, Jerry."

Unthinkingly, I ran my free hand through my own thinning hair.

"Yeah. I guess so."

"Your Mama might not have recognized you." He hadn't called her Mama since I was very small. I think he was retreating into memories just then. I couldn't blame him. I didn't want to be the one to yank him into the uncomfortable present.

The silence resumed.

Then he said, "It was just a stroke that killed her. Just a simple stroke. Like that." He snapped his fingers. This display was meant to comfort me. No, she didn't suffer from some hideous malformation unknown to science and melt away into putrescent slime. Very neat and tidy. Just a stroke.

I swallowed hard, and was about to say something.

"I'm sorry you missed the funeral," he said.

"I'm sorry too. There was a strike in Buenos Aires. I couldn't get a plane until yesterday afternoon."

And now, an absurdity so agonizing it was a torturer's stroke of genius. The old *Mister Ed* theme went rattling through my brain. It was all I could do not to sing aloud something about people yakety-yakking and wasting the time of day. But I didn't. Be thankful for small mercies. I wept, just a little. Father doubtless thought the tears were for Mama, and seemed moved.

We can't say the important things. Words fail us.

I sat on one of the plastic-protected chairs. In silence. For a long time. Outside, the sky darkened.

Gradually, very subtly, for all I knew he was still locked in his room in the attic, my brother was there, with us, impatient as always.

I had to say it at last. "How's Jeffrey, Dad?" There, I thought. Did it.

"He's still changing. Like the book said he would. I'm afraid of him, Jerry. I don't think he knows me anymore. I don't think he'll recognize you either."

But I'll have to try, remained unsaid. *You know that, Papa.*

*   *   *

I remembered that it had been on a winter evening much like this one, the year I was thirteen and Jeffrey was seventeen, that the two of us went outside together for what should have been the last time.

He'd shambled into my room, knocking over books, sending my portable record-player to the floor with a screech that guaranteed that my copy of *Sgt. Pepper's Lonely Hearts Club Band* was going to have to be replaced.

"Let's go out. And play. Please." He smelled particularly bad just then. His tusks gleamed and dripped with drool. He had to squeeze himself sideways to fit through the doorway. Something, probably a new, vestigial limb stirred underneath the extra-extra-large Philadelphia Eagles sweat-shirt he always wore.

I picked up, then unplugged the record player and set it on my desk. The record itself was so obviously ruined I could only drop it into the wastebasket.

For just a second, I was angry enough to hit him.

"Want to p-p-play." His eyes, sunken in his mottled face, were still my brother's eyes. I still knew him. Some of him, a little bit, was still that Jeffrey who had walked to school with me as recently as five years earlier, before he was taken out of school and all the kids started beating me up and teasing me, shouting, "You're brother's a retard and you are too!"

No, it wasn't that, of course. For a time, doctors came and said it was some rare and spectacular disease. One was even an Englishman from Merck. I didn't know what that meant. For the longest time I thought Merck was a place in England.

Then Mother wouldn't let them come anymore and wouldn't let Jeffrey go out of the house.

But tonight, she and Daddy were off somewhere. It might have been one of their periodic frenzies of church-going. They might have been off asking God to make Jeffrey normal again. *Take this cup away from me*, as the phrase went.

Even I knew it wasn't a matter of cups, or God's business. Jeffrey knew it too. I think that my parents were just as certain, but they still prayed, so they wouldn't give in to despair.

My brother shook his head violently from side to side, banging against the door frame with his teeth like an angry bull with its horns, gouging chunks out of the wood.

"Okay! Okay! I'm coming." I hurried to put on my hat, coat, and gloves, while he stirred and stamped. A stain spread down the front of his jogging pants and started to pour onto the floor. I'd clean that up later. I reached up and put my arm around his neck, to calm him. One of the huge tusks slid wetly against my cheek, but bristling with sharp edges and points from the endlessly intricate carvings he spent most of his time executing.

("Scrimshaw." He'd read that word in a book. "Scrim! Shaw!" like a football cheer, but sputtered, grunted. "Yes, carvings on the teeth of a whale," Mama said, then added, in one of her frenzied periods, "for you are Leviathan, the Great Beast.")

So we waded out into the still-falling snow, in the evening twilight, me all bundled up with long scarf trailing, a regular boy, and Jeffrey, still in his Eagles sweatshirt and jogging pants, barefoot...I would never have taken him out in broad daylight, no matter how much he wanted to play. No, I couldn't. But now, there was a certain thrill to it. He was my secret, the vast and potent magic I alone commanded...or so the game went.

We scrambled quickly across the narrow concrete strip that served as a common driveway for all the houses in our row, then I easily climbed over the fence – I had to find an opening for Jeffrey, who was too heavy – and slid, slightly out of control, down the embankment into the comforting security of Haverbrook Park itself, that not-very-large, hilly woodland which seemed endless as the night came on.

He was clumsier than ever before, crashing through the trees and briers, moving on all fours much of the time, but not on his knuckles like an ape, instead with his hands flat on the ground, leaving, huge, perfect hand prints in the snow.

He grunted and laughed and even clapped his enormous hands when he came to the stream, and wallowed right in, sitting in the frigid water, splashing. The cold didn't seem to bother him.

Carefully, I tried to cross on a log, but slipped, and found myself standing in water to my knees, my boots filled, the water so cold it burned before my legs went numb.

"Play!" Jeffrey sputtered, like a very small child, happy as he could be, like the mental retard the neighborhood kids always claimed he was.

But I knew better. I had always known better. Jeffrey merely enjoyed his frivolous moments, when he momentarily escaped those cares and fears he could not express by any means other than carving strange figures and letters on his nearly foot-long tusks.

I was glad for him, just then. I waded to the further bank. "Come on, Jeff," I said. "Let's play."

So we ran and climbed among the rocks and trees, wandering deeper and deeper into the park, as the land rose and the woods shut out the lights and noise of the city that surrounded us. We came, at last, to a series of stone terraces, high above the stream. Some people said they were man-made, that there had once been a forge there, back in the time of the Revolution. Certainly there were a lot of stories about that place.

On this particular night, as it had been some times before, it was *our* place alone, a secret we two brothers shared. We sat on the highest stones, in the darkness, hidden from the world. I was shivering all over then, clinging to Jeffrey for warmth; but in vain, because he wasn't warm, and felt cold and hard, like living metal beneath his soggy, half-frozen clothes.

"Fairy tale," he sputtered. That was his other truly childlike characteristic. He liked fairy tales, always had, since he was small, and the way to tell him one was to make him part of it, one of the characters.

"Once, long ago, in an old-time kingdom, there was a Beast that lived in the woods. That's you, Jeff. You're the Beast. That's not a bad thing to be, because the Beast is really a prince and he can do magic."

"And...what you?"

I shrugged. "I guess I'm the King's huntsman." I tried to laugh. "You don't want me to be *Beauty*, do you? I mean, that would be queer, like a girl, you know – "

"Does the huntsman kill the Beast?" For once he didn't sputter. The question was startling. He'd seen right through the tale.

I didn't know what to say. "Um, no. Of course not."

"What's the rest of the story then?"

"I think it's that the King got so angry with his oldest son – the Royal Wrath was something everyone was afraid of – and when the King was in his rage the ground shook, and there was lightning in the sky – and the King was so angry with his son that he put a curse on him, and the kingdom was cursed too, and the trees died, and the rivers dried up, and there was only silence afterward. Everyone went away, and they left the Beast alone, everyone except his brother, the younger prince who was not afraid of him. And – "

I started to cry then, because I was lying, because the story didn't go that way. It wasn't as simple as that. It was so unfair that we couldn't just be brothers and grow up together, like other kids did. I *didn't know* how the story would end and was afraid that it never would; not because of anything we'd done, or even because of anything Father had done in his Royal Wrath or Mother had in her prayerful frenzies. No, it was nobody's fault that our grandparents and great-grandparents and great-great-grandparents had come from someplace up north called Dunwich and had been named Whateley; and that someone had passed on from generation to generation an old book called the *Necronomicon*, and that some of the words Jeffrey carved on his teeth were in that book and Daddy could read them, but would never tell me what they said.

It wasn't fair that sometime back in the 1920s the Whateleys had tried a great Experiment and failed, but, somehow, that Experiment had worked its way down the years and through the bloodlines until it came out again in Jeffrey.

I cried because of all that, because it wasn't fair.

And my brother did the most extraordinary thing. He touched me gently on the back of the neck, almost as if he were stroking me – if anybody else had done it, it would have been queer – and he told *me* a story, struggling for the words around the impediment of his ungainly tusks. I didn't understand very much of it, but it was about how the Beast was not really a monster after all, but part of a different family, and how "Those of the Air," as Jeffrey put it, would come someday and take him to a better place, maybe another planet. I couldn't make that out. There were a lot of words in the story that were just buzzing and spitting and barking sounds.

"Does the younger prince get to come too?" I asked.

"No. Blood of Them in him, but not enough. He can just barely see them."

And we sat for a long time in the darkness after that, and it seemed indeed – I was certain I imagined what I saw, that it was a kind of dream – that the wind circled around us again and again, with a whispered whoosh like a fleet of huge trucks passing, and sometimes I could see shapes among the trees, distorted bodies, and luminous faces floating among the branches. They called out to Jeffrey, and he answered back, in a language I didn't know.

I nearly froze to death. Jeffrey had to carry me back to the house. He smashed in the back door because he couldn't open it. Father was waiting for him, and in his Royal Wrath beat Jeffrey with a shovel, and locked him in the attic room, and never let him out again. I went to the hospital for frostbite and missed some school, and later, I could only talk to my brother through the locked door when I slid his meals in through the slot Father had installed. Jeffrey didn't answer back much, and I never got to tell him any more of the story of the two princes.

* * *

"You go upstairs and rest for a while, Son," my father said. "You've had a long trip up from South America. I'll fix us a little something in the kitchen. Then you come down again."

I don't know how he thought I'd want to rest, or linger here at all, considering what the inevitable outcome must be, but *he*, I think, wanted to delay it just a bit longer, and I granted him the courtesy of this reprieve. Maybe he just wanted to be a father again, one last time.

So, silently, I went upstairs, into my old bedroom. I flicked on the light and saw that absolutely nothing had changed since the day, when I was twenty-three, I had stormed out of the house. There was still a 1982 newspaper on the floor, under the dust. And a pair of dirty socks.

I sat down on the bed and just stared into the indeterminate distance of the room, which was not a matter of physical space at all: at the bookshelves, even the model airplanes which had dangled from the ceiling since my childhood.

And, irony of ironies: the sleeve for *Sgt. Pepper's Lonely Hearts*

Club Band was still on the shelf in front of me. I had never gotten around to replacing the record.

My hand found something on the bed, under the covers, something which had *not* need there before: a leather-bound photo album. I recognized some of the pictures, from family outings, graduations, and the like. I paged through it with a mixture of dull curiosity, then something almost like anger, then just exhausted sadness. The pictures had been altered, mutilated with a ball-point pen. My own image had sometimes been made into that of a prince, with crown and flowing robes and a sword, sometimes the huntsman, with a gun or bow-and-arrows and a Robin Hood cap. Once, my eyebrows had been raised and I'd acquired long fingernails and a pigtail – a comic Chinaman. I had no idea why.

Mother's image had been the object of anger, the eyes and sometimes the whole face gouged out. She'd been given ass's ears more than once, and there was even an enormous posterior drawn in the sky over her wedding picture. There she was, a bride, on the church steps, her face scraped away, and it was raining shit.

The final picture in the book was one of father, exhausted, reclining on a plastic-covered sofa. I think it had actually been taken one Christmas, as he snoozed after all the preparations were done. But now there were wires going into his arms and sides, and a carefully-rendered monitor on the wall above him, the line on the screen a zigzag, flattening out.

Father in Intensive Care, dying.

The one truly frightening thing was that I didn't know if this was Jeffrey's work, which it should have been – but how had he known I was coming and how had he gotten out to place the book here for me to find? – or Papa's own.

Above me, something stirred, then hit the upstairs floor hard, again and again, as if stamping its hooves.

God help me, I thought of that old TV sitcom theme: *A horse is a horse* –

And fully, and deeply, I wept, lying there on the bed, amid the dust and papers and old laundry.

* * *

Father and I ate in silence, badly cooked eggs and bacon. He couldn't look me in the eye. He stared at his plate, swirling his fork around in the grease.

I was thinking in clichés. I should have felt that there was so much I had to say to him: that I, his estranged son, truly loved him after all, that I wished our family could be together again, like old times, the whole routine. But there, sitting with him, I couldn't think of anything to say at all. I was empty. I'd cried my last tears on the bedspread upstairs, and that was the end of that.

Two floors above us, the pounding was louder, insistent.

"Come on, Son," he said at last. "We've got to finish this."

So I followed him upstairs that last time. He paused at the first landing, staring into my bedroom, where I'd left the light on and the photo album out on the bed. Then he turned into his own room. I went to follow him. He held me back.

"Wait."

He still had to have his little secret, his final one. All right. He could have it. I waited patiently while he rustled around in the dark. I could only imagine that the bedroom, too, hadn't been touched, that my mother's things were exactly as she'd left them. It sounded like her closet that Father was rummaging in.

He came out with something wrapped in a garbage bag. Even before I felt the heavy, iron-bound covers through the plastic, I knew what it was: the ancient *Necronomicon*.

"You'll have to study," was all he said.

That was almost the very last thing he said to me, ever. He flicked on a light. We went up the attic steps in silence. He indicated that I should be the one to remove the heavy, five-pointed stone sigil that leaned against the door of the attic room. By now the smell was almost overpowering, the stench of garbage and excrement and something that almost might have been burning, sulfurous, vile, but ultimately unidentifiable. Why the neighbors didn't have the Board of Health or the police in long ago was beyond me.

There was no sound at all from behind that door, as I dragged the heavy stone away, as Father undid the padlocks and slid the bolts back.

He opened the door, and I took the first step inside, my feet stirring what must have been old steak and pork bones.

"Jeff? You there?"

Father grabbed me from behind with surprising strength, his arm in a choke hold around my neck. He hurled me back, across the tiny landing, against the opposite wall. He held me there with both hands, and for once his eyes met mine and his face was utterly, utterly inscrutable. I could make out the King with his Royal Wrath, and Papa, exhausted beyond words, despairing, wanting only for it all to end, and more. Possibly he wanted to explain it all to me, or ask my forgiveness, or merely wish that things had turned out differently. I don't know. He was angry, sad, firm, and stoically uncaring all at once.

All he said to me was, "No. Wait here. It was supposed to be your mother. Now it *has* to be me."

"Father, I – ?"

He squeezed my hands tight over the *Necronomicon*, then turned from me and went, meekly but with no hesitation, into the dark room.

As a final offering. Because Jeffrey was grown up now, and it was time.

In the instant of silence that followed, I found myself plagued with another comic, irrelevant thought, a memory of a Gahan Wilson cartoon showing a puffy-faced young man confronting his seated, frog-faced father in what must have been the great hall of an old English manor. Portraits of frog-faced ancestors lined the walls, and the caption read, "Son, now that you're of age, it's about time I told you about the old family curse."

About time.

In the room, my father was screaming. But I knew he wouldn't want me to come in.

The screaming stopped. Something heavy and wet dropped to the floor. Then I heard a sucking sound, like an electric pump struggling with a clogged drain, and after that a series of snaps, which I knew were bones breaking.

Again, silence. The smell grew even worse.

I knew what I had to do. There was only one possibility left.

"Jeffrey," I said. "It's me. It's Jerry. Come out. I want to tell you a story. Remember?"

And from within the darkness came my brother's voice, "Play?"

"Yes," I said. "Let's go out and play."

Holding the book, I backed down the steps, and he came out onto the landing, whimpering a little as he brushed against the five-pointed stone; for he had grown so huge that he could not help but touch it.

He didn't wear clothes anymore. His whole body, even his tusks, had turned a greenish-black, the color of tarnished metal; but his muscles and numerous limbs I couldn't quite make out seemed more like a huge tangle of ropes come alive. He stumbled and thumped down the stairs, squeezing between the walls, one surprisingly human hand grasping the railing. His head, on top, seemed almost an irrelevancy, like a basketball floating on frothing water. But I could still see his eyes, and they were my brother's eyes.

Of course his passage made complete havoc of the immaculate living room. It was only there, in the better light, that I realized that Jeffrey had an extra mouth where his chest should be, vertical, like an insect's mouth, lined with needle-teeth. Praying-Mantis claws held the remains of our father firmly in place. Jeffrey streaked the living room, and the kitchen, and the back stairs, with slime and blood and the debris of smashed furniture.

Outside, in the darkness, in the swirling snow, I coaxed him through the fence, into the park. We waded through the stream once again, as he had when we were boys, and it was just as cold now, and once again I didn't care. This time I didn't fall, though. I clutched the plastic-wrapped *Necronomicon* tightly under one arm.

"Play," Jeffrey said, clapping his hands. "Play."

Once more we climbed the hillside, in the darkness, Jeffrey shoving the trees aside, making a terrible racket – but no one disturbed us – until we reached the terraces.

And in our secret place, we sat together, and I told him the rest of the story of the Prince and the Beast, how the younger brother released the elder from the castle's dungeon, how the Beast devoured the King, as was only fitting; and the King's guards fled in terror at their approach, and the two of them retreated far, far into the forest, where no huntsman could ever follow, until they reached the secret and eternal land of the beasts, where animals spoke in their own languages, and no human being was ever admitted.

But because the Prince was the Beast's brother, he was allowed to the very threshold of that land. He could see into it through the thick under-brush, just for an instant, as the leaves parted when the Beast and those who had come for him went back inside. The other animals did not kill the Prince, and, knowing that he would not betray them, they allowed him to leave.

"Is that the end of the story?" said Jeffrey.

"I don't know. I don't think so." I should have been sobbing. That would have been right. But I had run out of tears. As before, when I sat with Father in the kitchen during his last meal, I felt only empty and had nothing more to say.

Then They of the Air finished the story, whispering to Jeffrey in their own language. I saw them, clearly this time, huge, winged, impossible shapes with fiery faces, half like smoke, swirling in the night sky, weaving between the trees, their passage a great whirlwind. Branches flew. Trees creaked and swayed. Jeffrey, wild with excitement, leapt up, doing a kind of dance on the hilltop, howling and hooting, stamping his several enormous feet. I was irrelevant to all this, like a pigeon that's wandered into a parade. I could have been crushed. I scrambled down the hillside, out of my brother's way, and looked up just once as a particularly brilliant flash of lightning tore the sky apart. My eyes were dazzled. I couldn't be sure. But Jeffrey seemed transformed once more, into something utterly indescribable and powerful, with wings that reached out to touch the horizons. He and the others filled the sky, rising up.

And then there was just me, sitting alone in the cold and the dark on the hillside, still clutching the plastic-wrapped book I didn't know how to read, unable to understand how the story had turned out.

The Throwing Suit

JEFFREY QUILT'S PAINTINGS were muted, desolate things: curiously disturbing patterns of grays and browns mostly, with a very rare burst of some bright color so brilliant it came as a shock. "Etudes" he called his works. They sold well; they were affordable. I am sure he made a comfortable living from them, for all his house and studio always seemed on the verge of being condemned by either the Board of Health, the building inspectors, or both.

"The artistic temperament," he used to joke, "makes a wonderful excuse for many sorts of otherwise unacceptable behavior, including simple laziness."

"But far more, too," I said, on this particular occasion. "Far, far more."

"You're quite right," he said as he led me through the obstacle course of the living room, amid boxes of papers, old canvases, a broken TV set which now served as a repository for old and sometimes only half-emptied TV dinner trays, and boxes upon boxes of old, lurid paperback novels and magazines he always called his "reference library," but which, as far as I could tell, bore no relevance whatever to his painting.

"For who," I went on in this mock-pretentious mode, "can possibly know the soul of a true artist?"

He had reached the base of the steps, and he turned to me, sharply. The look on his face was puzzling. At first I thought he was actually angry with me, and I wondered what I'd said wrong. Then, for less than a second he seemed *afraid*, as if remembering for something, or even *listening*. I listened too, but all I heard was the strident chirping of Fido, his pet parakeet and sole house mate.

At last he laughed, not very convincingly. "I suppose that is why we'll never know the reason Hemingway cut off his ear."

I said nothing as we ascended, past the strange little miniatures that lined the stairwell, pictures of not-quite cute animals and animal-headed humans doing frequently less than cute things to one another amid teetering, vaguely medieval cityscapes.

The entire second storey of the house was devoted to his "garret," four rooms worth. Here was one of the great treasure-repositories of the United States, little-known by mainstream art critics, but to the devotee a curious mixture of the Louvre and King Tut's tomb. Small oils were hung everywhere, on all the walls of all the rooms, on the doors, in the hall, in the closet-sized bathroom. ("I am considering the expansion potential of the ceiling," he said virtually every time I visited him.) Still more paintings stood upright in boxes in the middle of the floor.

As always, he followed me around wraithlike as I browsed, making his inevitable joke about discounts and saving his "admirers" gallery fees and sales tax. Then he went on, as he sometimes did, to philosophize upon *de morbis artificum*, the artist's sedentary ways and the morbidity that often attended such an existence.

Over the years I had acquired three Jeffrey Quilt oil paintings, and now, on this blustery December evening, after a good deal of searching, I believed I had found a fourth: one to match the season, a drab but intricate depiction of a costumed, ghostly figure seen from behind, looking out the window of a tower on what seemed to be a winter evening exactly like the present one.

I lifted it out of a box from between two others and held it up to Quilt.

"Ah, *The Throwing Suit*. There is a story behind that one. A truly horrible story."

Once more he seemed to be *listening*. Then he looked at me, awaiting my indication that he should continue.

"I will buy the painting," I said, "on the strict condition that the story isn't true. I don't want a painting with a bad history."

"Like the Hope Diamond."

"Yes, like that."

"Then I am afraid that I cannot sell the painting to you," he said evenly. Come, there are others in the next room which may interest you, a new series I call *Revenants of the Living*."

He gestured to the door. But I couldn't stop staring at the ghostly figure. It must have been a trick of the light, but the shrouded man (I think it was a man) looked smaller now, more overwhelmed by shadows, and by the hugeness of the room in which he stood. The point of view was perhaps from a doorway, and at the full length of the room this figure stood gazing out another doorway, or perhaps a large window, at...what? Only the foreground details were clear: chipping paint, stains, exposed and rotting boards behind broken plaster. As far as I could make out, the standing figure's costume made no sense at all. It was sort of a shroud-like coat, with some of the characteristics of a straight-jacket, only with too many straps and arms.

A *throwing suit* he had called it.

"Now you've got me curious," I said. "You *must* tell me the story."

"Very well, I will, but only on the *strict condition* that you buy the painting. Only then."

Adamant, he stared at me until I agreed – which I was reluctant to do since I'm more than a little superstitious. I handed him a check. Then we went downstairs into the kitchen, he cleared off two chairs, and we sat over paper cups of Pabst Blue Ribbon while he told me how autobiographical this particular painting was.

"That's half the reason I want to get rid of it," he said. Just then the wind whistled through the back door. The sound startled him. He knocked over the half-empty bottle, then righted it, but didn't bother to clean up the mess before beginning his story.

*   *   *

I have my own little audience, *Quilt declared*, consisting of aficionados of a similar stripe to myself, who collect my work and have troubled themselves to make personal contact with me.

Five years ago, a collector of my work, a friend, put me in touch with a wealthy man with a great interest in otherworldly phenomena. I hasten to emphasize – I believe it is important – that I never saw my patron in the flesh. I met his go-betweens, servants, employees or whatever, and I spoke with him on the phone a few times. I got the impression that he was a recluse, perhaps a cripple. He offered me a commission. The amount was such that I didn't ask very many questions. For this extravagant sum, I was to execute an oil painting of a house, a property he owned in rural Chester County. Haunted, needless to say. I emphasized that my artwork is seldom pleasant to look at, and this seemed only to encourage him in his belief that he had chosen the right artist.

"For reasons of health," he said, "I must avoid this ghostly haven. But I am intensely eager to know what it *feels* like to be there. The video-tapes I've already had made were unremarkable; you'd never know it was a haunted house. I dismissed a local portraitist who proposed to work from photographs: he insisted on completing the painting in his studio. He could not possibly capture – I suppose you would call it – the authentic atmosphere of the place without being there all the time he worked. Therefore I have chosen you, Jeffrey Quilt, an artist who specializes in macabre subject-matter. If you accept, you will stay in the house and work there. The kitchen will be stocked with food. The electricity will be on. When the painting is complete, you will call me. There is a telephone on the first floor. My man will come for the painting within the hour. Further, although I don't insist on it, I would appreciate it very much if you would call me periodically to describe your impressions."

"You are a man whose interests seems to mirror my own," I said, almost frivolously.

Very grimly, he said, "Hear me out. If we are to proceed, then you must agree to one *strict condition:* in order for me to be sure you are not working from photographs, a member of my staff will personally drive you to the house and lock you inside. Ten thousand dollars shall be yours, Jeffrey Quilt, if you abide by these terms and if you have a finished painting at the end of your stay."

The wealthy man went on to explain that the house was in a remote area ("No neighbors for miles in any direction") and that the windows were boarded up ("To discourage vandals!").

I was intrigued, to say the least. An authentic *haunted* house. This was my métier after all. And working from photographs, I had to agree, would sacrifice the whole point.

I agreed. My patron insisted we begin at once. I began to pack my bags and painting supplies. A half an hour later the doorbell rang, and there was the millionaire's man, in a chauffeur's uniform no less, but I soon understood that he was more than just a driver.

"My employer insists that the painting be utterly *realistic,*" this fellow said. "Nothing made up. Nothing fanciful."

"Certainly not. I have a reputation to maintain. Like a certain distin-guished predecessor, I paint what I see."

"…And the completion date of the painting?"

I hedged. "Perhaps a week. Longer if I need it. But I must insist on a down-payment in any case."

He looked at me sternly, but was ready for this. He drew a fat envelope out of his pocket.

"Would twenty-five hundred dollars be acceptable?"

* * *

A few minutes later I was the passenger in a Lincoln Continental, whizzing through the Pennsylvania countryside as twilight came on. My companion stared at the road ahead as if determined to pretend I didn't exist.

"It's a shame your boss can't come along," I said. "This really sounds like his kind of thing."

The driver said nothing.

"I *said* I wish I could meet your employer."

The response was one of barely controlled rage. "It is not possible. Because of an infirmity, he is unable to travel."

"So, what does he do with his time?"

The veins on his forehead stood out as he pondered my question.

"He studies...mysteries."

"You mean like Ellery Queen and Sherlock Holmes?"

"*Sir*, if you are unable to take this any more seriously than you seem to show, I shall be forced to tell my employer that he has made the wrong choice for a painter."

"Now wait a minute," I said. "I'm your man, all right. I just want to know, what do you mean by mysteries?"

"You would not understand."

"Try me."

He all but spat the word. "Gnosticism."

It was hopeless. Once or twice further during the ride I tried to initiate conversation with him, but was curtly rebuffed. The driver was a complete mystery to me, his manner, both bland beyond my ability to describe and at the same time definitely hostile, was offensive in the extreme. Worse, it made no sense. It was as if service to his employer had all but erased him, and what remained was not his own personality, but an extension of his superior's, those parts of the inner mind the outer shell of custom and propriety keep hidden. My very nearness seemed to be an unforgivable violation of privacy.

As we drove, the countryside grew ever more desolate: the dun-colored, sloping hillsides stubbled with dead cornstalks, the occasional weathered house with its western-facing windows faintly gleaming in the last glimmer of sunlight. The December landscape and darkening sky were a lesson for me, a reminder of seasonal mortality, of mortalities everywhere.

I cherished such scenes. I was eager to paint.

Down a sloping country road we continued until we finally arrived, gravel rattling in an unpaved driveway; we pulled up in front of a solid-looking stone and wood farmhouse surrounded by milkweed.

The driver helped me with my luggage. He let the motor run. I stood in the gathering darkness and gazed up at what was more than a simple farmhouse.

"What a melange!" I said aloud, eyeing the weird combination of architectural styles: a round tower with a conical roof (an allusion to a castle or a chateau), a broad, single-span porch supported on two pairs of columns, the spindlework and detailing on the porch an even more curious mixture of foliate faces, serpents, Colonial Revival Tuscan columns, Romanesque revival with Prussian inflections; an awkward, uneasy blend. "The architect must have been *on* something. No wonder the place is haunted."

"The house was built in 1892," the driver sniffed as if that explained something. He jammed the key into the door, turned it. The door creaked open.

"Once you are inside, you are to call my employer."

"I thought he only wanted my impressions, and it was optional."

"Those are his *specific* instructions, sir."

Shuffling inside with my gear, I found myself in a large, unlit foyer. I couldn't see much, but the driver flicked on a switch with something like familiarity.

"Mr. Quilt," he intoned as he stood in the doorway. "I am to remind you that you forfeit the commission if you try to leave on your own." (Here, for the first time, a little, ingratiating smile.) "Leaving would be difficult in any event, for the windows are boarded up, the door is sturdy, and there are no tools."

As per our agreement, he ransacked my luggage and materials in search of a camera. While watching him do this, I became apprehensive. "What if there's a fire?"

"There is a volunteer fire company in the nearest town. You could make the call, then run up to the tower, which has a balcony, or perhaps you might consider it a porch, just under the roof. Wait there. It would be a simple matter to fetch you down with a ladder."

"Have you ever been up there?"

"Alas, the view is best appreciated by someone with the sensibility possessed by you or…my master."

Another strange facet to this strange character: for the first time his voice seemed tinged with *regret*. And for the first time he referred to his boss as his master. But things were too hurried for me to question him further. Satisfied I had not smuggled a camera along, he smiled again – a mocking smile – then let himself out. I heard the key turning in the keyhole, and a minute later the car rumbling away.

Alone in the house, I admired the furniture, the antique fixtures. There is the comforting but false belief that by possessing things – books, curios, paintings – we can somehow arrest the flow of time. A treasured photograph seems to freeze a scene or a loved one like an insect in amber; there it is on the shelf, never fading. I thought that this was what the wealthy man had done. Perhaps he was dying of some strange disease. Therefore he had purchased a house where the stream of time did not flow, where the dust and the smells and the passing hours were utterly stagnant, *here*.

It was an odd notion. Almost at once, I got out my sketchbook and began to draw as I wandered from room to room in the downstairs of the house: here a drapery, there a chair, again a coffin-shaped grandfather clock which had long since stopped ticking. I thought: Time is the artist's silent assistant. The artist stands back and watches time at work; as the pencil strokes accumulate, the sketch seems to fill in by itself. There are seasons in each moment.

The phone was ringing. I continued sketching, unmindful of it. All at once the ringing stopped. Only the sudden silence alerted me. Only then did it occur to me that I was hours overdue with my first phone call.

Behind the telephone was a huge pier mirror. A slip of paper with phone numbers on it had been taped to the mirror. As I dialed, I winced at the reflection of myself, at the daydreaming expression of a man who took no notice of time except to rhapsodize about it in morbid reveries.

My call finally went through. An enfeebled voice answered, my patron's without a doubt, but fainter, muttering something about the lateness of the hour and my discourtesy. But his words faded away as I thought about the essential quality of this mansion, about the compost of the days here, gathering slowly like falling leaves the rich humus of hours.

"I lost track of time," I heard myself saying over the phone.

"Quilt! Tell me what you see!"

I tried to describe the vaulting foyer, the spiral staircase winding to the second floor. I mentioned the sketches I had made so far. "I haven't been upstairs yet," I said. Then I told him about the kitchen, which was frightening only in its banality.

"Have you located the *bad place* in the house?"

I joked: "I *am* the bad place."

"Eh –?"

" *'Which way I fly is Hell; myself am Hell....'* "

"Have you found it or not?" he demanded.

Relenting, I suggested that the *bad place* might be upstairs. My sketches thus far were rather like seismographic recordings of a quakeless land: no 'jolts' yet.

"It would be a lot easier," I complained, "if you'd stop playing games with me and just *tell* me where the hauntings occurred." I noticed a closet behind me, reflected in the pier mirror.

"As I've already explained, Quilt, I do not wish to plant any suggestion in your mind which could lead to bias."

"For instance, I am in the kitchen. Across from me is a closet – "

"Which should be firmly sealed shut."

"Actually, the door is ajar."

"What?"

I walked across to the closet, trailing phone wire. Even as I did the door swung outward, releasing air that smelled of damp earth long confined.

"It's opening," I said. "The door is open all the way now. Is this it? Am I getting warmer?"

"No. Stay away from that closet, Quilt. That's an order. *Stay away.* It's off limits. The door may swing shut on you. It can't be opened from the inside. You would suffocate. There's no one to hear you."

Even as he spoke I nudged the door open more. Inside was what looked like a canvas costume drooped over a black portfolio. I saw a colorfully paint-smeared box on the floor.

"The door's completely open," I said innocently. "Is that a box of pastels on the floor?"

"Close the door, Quilt. Close it *now.*"

I knelt down and opened the box. "Art supplies. And some kind of artist's smock with a hood. I've never seen anything quite like it."

"Jeffrey, please. Leave that closet alone."

I handled the smock. The weave was very coarse, like sailcloth. It was yellowed with great age, but still very strong. Its purpose and design I couldn't immediately figure out. There were a lot of buckles in places that didn't make any sense, and more straps than there were buckles. Strangest of all, the hood did not open to allow the wearer any view out at all, or even breathing room. What I took to be the front had a solid oval of metal riveted into it, like a heavy, featureless mask.

"This is weird," I said. "It's sort of a straight-jacket. It's very old – "

"God *damn* you Quilt! The age has no bearing on your assignment. Leave that closet alone and concentrate on your painting."

Just then an almost inexplicable impulse came over me. While little admonitions were spewing out of the telephone – grumbles and threats and pleadings from a probable invalid many miles away ("Those items are personal property. They are irreplaceable. You have no right.") – it seemed to me that the only possible course of action was to *put the smock on.*

I slid it over my head. The smell of old canvas was overwhelming. And there was something else, distinctly unpleasant, like rotting meat. The feel of the cloth, too, was quite nasty, at first as rough as steel-wool, then warm and soft and firm, as if the thing were alive, as if I were inside a huge and toothless mouth which clamped down on me harder and harder.

I struggled to breathe. Somewhere, very far away, a voice was screaming, "Put it away Quilt! Put it away!"

I still had the phone receiver with me, inside the smock, or bag, or whatever it was.

"...the throwing suit...." he seemed to be saying. "...damn you, Quilt. Damn you."

My mind wasn't right then. My perceptions were distorted. It seemed to take hours, and only with the utmost concentration of will could I wriggle out of the thing, as if indeed it were a dark mouth filled with slime, holding me tighter and tighter.

Then I was sitting on the kitchen floor, the 'throwing suit' crumpled in my lap. I fumbled for the phone.

"Hello....?" I gasped for breath.

"Put it *back*, Quilt."

Without hesitation, I obeyed, and kicked the closet door shut.

"If it will be any comfort to you, I could always nail the door shut."

"There aren't any tools, Quilt. Remember?"

"I could block it with something heavy."

"Yes, you do that Quilt. Then get back to your painting." He excused himself, pleading that his blood pressure was soaring, and hung up.

I sat there for a long time, bewildered. Bingo, I thought. The spectral seismograph has recorded its first tremor. Time, indeed, seemed to stand still. I sat, trying to focus my thoughts, feeling vaguely ill. I don't know how long it was. Eventually a full bladder forced me to get up and find the bathroom.

*   *   *

I slept late the following morning and only fitfully attempted breakfast. I couldn't remember any dreams, but was left with the impression of having dreamed. Only a hint remained, a pseudo-memory of endless grayness, like a world filled with ash.

I spent much of the afternoon wandering through the first and second storeys of the house, sketching, absorbing the congested stillness that is the characteristic of such places: the curious density of rooms left unoccupied, of objects untouched and unused for decades. Stale-smelling sheets covered the furniture and gray dust – yes, like that in my forgotten dream – covered everything. Amid this ghostly furniture I sat and sketched, then rose, went to another room, sketched again, everywhere stirring up swirls of dust. Sunlight sliced through the cracks of the boarded windows. I savored the motes that sparkled in the brilliant beams.

My attention wandered. I mused on time and death and the enigma of my unseen patron. None of my sketches amounted to anything. Frustrated, I gave up and started rummaging. I found a cache of old magazines in a trunk in one of the rooms, mystery pulps from the 1930s, *Police Gazette* from the '40s. I have no idea how they got there, but they were just the thing for the moment. I sat paging through them happily, for hours. At times I need pure trash, to rescue me from the sublime. Life is short and Art is long, too long, sometimes.

In truth, all the rooms I had been in were harmless and even agreeable. They radiated a certain antique charm. But then it somehow became completely clear to me, as I sat reading the pulp magazines, that my true subject matter, the *bad place* which would earn my ten thousand dollars, was not in the closet below, but, inevitably, above me, on the unexplored third floor, in the tower.

So my ambition and plain greed propelled me, and the fascination of the prospect drove me, but my better judgment – call it my artist's sense of proportion, of *form* – bade me wait until the evening, when the light through the window-slats deepened to red and twisted into the musty carpet at sharp angles. Then, and only then, would it be time for me to ascend.

For it is in the fading of the day, when the last traces of sunlight remind us of death, that hauntings manifest themselves. Somehow I was utterly sure. My patron was paying me for my impressions, and *that* was my impression.

But first I went down into the kitchen and got the "throwing suit" out of the closet. I was afraid of it – yes, afraid of an inanimate thing of canvas and metal – but it was again my impression – I *knew* – that I would need it, that despite my patron's hope that I could draw the essence of this place out with sheer artistic perception, the "throwing suit" was the key to the whole puzzle.

Haunted, I had been assured this house was. *…I hear there are such things. They hold the talk of spirits, their mirth and sorrowings.*

No, merely silent. As I searched the antique chambers of the third floor, I found nothing worthy of my brush. I made a few sketches, but only of old rooms, atmospheric but devoid of the resonating *torment* which makes a true haunted place.

It came to me that my commission was at stake, that if I didn't find anything more definite, I would have to fabricate some strangeness which would surely fail to satisfy my patron.

He knew what he wanted. He just wasn't telling me. He was waiting for me to find it myself, so he could *recognize* it.

I still could not discern his motives. He was no *connoisseur.* I was sure of that. My impression of him, over the phone and through the actions of his intermediaries, was of a greedy, grasping, perhaps desperate man, but insensitive to the point of vulgarity. He was a man who had *lost* something, perhaps, and was expecting me to find it.

Still it puzzled me that he did not come here himself, even if he were an invalid, even if he had to be carried. A painting, no matter how brilliant, could only be a second-hand thing, a sensation conveyed rather than experienced directly.

Why had he even purchased this house?

Filled with questions, seeking answers, seeking, let me admit it, something *horrible* which would inspire a suitably impressive "haunted house" painting, I did the one thing I knew I had to: I put the "throwing suit" on again.

The smell was not nearly as bad, as if the thing were accustomed to me. I stood, more puzzled than afraid as it slithered over me, as some of the buckles seemed to fasten themselves of their own accord, as the sleeves found my arms and the straps bound my arms tightly to my sides. I thought briefly, *How am I going to paint anything tied up like this?* but the thought passed, as did the sensation of being restricted. All was numbness and I was floating in the dark; and it occurred to me that the real purpose of this device might not be restraint, that it was instead the Victorian equivalent of a sensory-deprivation tank, into which one could withdraw to contemplate the inner mysteries –

Then the metal oval settled over my face. I had a hand free somehow. I explored the mask, as if through gloves, and it was, as I had recalled, featureless and solid; *yet I could see through it.*

I did not question. At first there were only drifting globules of light before my eyes, but then I could see, clearly, the twilit staircase that led into the attic and into the tower. There was something *wrong* about this vision. It was all shades of gray, utterly devoid of color, and devoid of most textures, like a crude attempt to shade in the world with a lead pencil.

Somehow I stumbled up the stairs. The dust there was so rancid that I was grateful for my awkward costume, for it filtered the air. I bumped into a mummified bat, a leathery, pendulant thing. At no time did I feel afraid of the supernatural, of ghosts and hauntings and monsters from the dark, for inside the "throwing suit" I was curiously immune from such influences.

I came to a circular room which had to be the main chamber of the tower. I saw that it had once been set up as an artist's studio. A canvas still stood on an easel. Something had been painted there, or attempted, but I could only make out random daubings of gray and black; no colors at all.

What little light there was came from skylights set in the ceiling, and from a curtain, through which gray light strained.

I moved toward the curtain. The easel behind me crashed to the floor. I turned back, dully, and only slowly figured out that one of the trailing straps of my suit, something like a three-pronged grappling hook, had caught the easel by one of its legs.

The curtains parted for me of their own accord. Or perhaps it was the wind. The porch was much larger than I'd imagined. I was puzzled that I hadn't noticed it at all from the outside when I'd arrived. But nothing seemed frightening while I wore the suit, somehow. Unanswered questions I was content to leave unanswered.

I stumbled into a vase; a drowned squirrel poured out.

I stood in the open air, unassailable in a stiff breeze, surveying the leaden December landscape.

No, it wasn't even that. It was like a aquatint by Paul Klee, a world stripped of even the most essential details, barely there at all, flat as a map, without real life. The only features at all were leafless trees twitching into a white sky like blind optic nerves.

But where was the horror?

Even as I stood there, gazing, I was answered.

The horror was sheer emptiness, a vast emptiness, a sky without even stars, a world without even dust, decayed beyond all possibility of decay, still, silent, eternal.

The horror was that I was drawn inexorably to that place, by some force I could not explain, by the perversion of my own will, by the writhing action of the "throwing suit" itself, and ultimately by a kind of *lust*.

I tried to scream, but my mouth was filled with cloth. I tried to turn away, but my body seemed floating in a gray haze. I looked out, through the metal mask, onto that ultimate *death*, the death of sensation and experience, a death beyond the cessation of life. I was able to fold my knees, to make my legs buckle.

But the "throwing suit" dragged me on of its own volition. Helplessly I wriggled like a huge, enshrouded worm, to the edge of the porch, and up, over the stone railing, then down, into space.

I was falling, it seemed forever. There were no points of reference, only nausea, a feeling of weightlessness, of no longer having a body.

For an instant I thought I saw something moving among the trees. I wasn't afraid. It was a flash of hope. What a relief to encounter any animate creature, any being at all, among such devouring emptiness.

I tried to call out once more, but my voice was muffled.

Yet the thing heard me, and answered, and drew nearer.

I heard it, its voice fainter than the wind, calling my name.

Jeffrey Quilt, here I am, it seemed to say.

I could almost make out a form, shoulders, arms, but not really. I had to imagine them, to fabricate.

But I could see the face, an old man's face, pocked, shriveled, wrinkled, twisted with cruelty and greed and desperate, almost pathetic terror.

Help me, it said. *Bring me back, into death, at least into clean death. Damn you, Quilt*, it said. *I'll keep you here with me, forever. You deserve it. I cannot weep*, it said. *Even that is forbidden me.*

As I watched the face decayed into a bare skull no thicker than gray, dirty paper; a dull red glow throbbed within, lighting it like a pulsating paper lantern.

Jeffrey Quilt –

It touched me. I felt frigid fingers on my cheeks, closing behind my head.

Jeffrey Quilt –

I *recognized* the voice then. That was my *impression*, for which I was to be so richly paid.

I knew that I had at last met my patron, there, in the *bad place*.

*   *   *

My recollections beyond this point are confused. I cannot say what it was precisely that provoked me to terror, thence to action. Perhaps it was the prospect of remaining in this void forever. Perhaps it was the way the apparition caressed my forehead *lovingly* while alternately threatening and pleading.

Somehow I struggled, and sensation returned. I felt the restraints of the suit and fought against them, desperately, as if far more than my life depended on escape.

And I felt myself sliding free, the abrasive cloth tearing at my face and arms and thighs as if I were completely unprotected, naked.

I was far less afraid of falling three and more storeys from the tower balcony than I was of remaining inside the suit.

I was fortunate. My hands caught in the various straps and I dangled in the air, as I swung back and forth, scraping against the stone of the tower's outer wall. Fortunately, too, I somehow managed to climb up the outside of the "throwing suit," grasping the straps, then the trailing cord that led to the grappling hook, and at last the porch railing, *all the while with my eyes tightly closed.*

I crawled through the curtain, then lay still on the studio floor, gasping for breath, exhausted.

Downstairs the phone was ringing endlessly. I just lay there and listened to it ring. The sound was comforting, as was the simple sensation of a solid floor beneath me.

It was only after a very long time that I was able to go downstairs, answer the phone, and tell my patron that I had failed, that there would be no painting.

He sent driver for me. But before the man arrived I screwed up all my courage and returned to the tower room, and even to the porch. I stood there, looking out into the darkness, the "throwing suit" still dangling from the railing before me. I saw only the normal winter sky, and the Pennsylvania countryside. Then I noticed headlights coming up the driveway and I hurried downstairs again.

* * *

"My master sincerely hoped," the chauffeur said, "that you would be able to rely entirely on your artistic skills and sensibilities, and avoid the temptation of the throwing suit, which, as you have seen, proved so disastrous for him." He did not accuse; and he was not speculating. He merely knew.

I made no reply.

As we left, he eyed me – ironically, I think – and said, "You are not the first."

"Not the first," I said wearily.

"Only my master is the first. He was the first and only inhabitant of this house."

My foggy brain could not put the pieces together. "Wait a minute. That's...no, you must be mistaken. 1892. That would make your boss at least a hundred."

"My master was elderly when he built the house," the driver said. "He was seventy when he began what he called his *project*. He is now one hundred and sixty-seven years of age. His problem, Sir, which he had hoped that you would solve, is that he is unable to die."

* * *

Jeffrey Quilt stopped speaking. I sat there in the half-lit kitchen. My beer had lost all its foam. The house was quiet, but for occasional pingings and creakings. Even the parakeet was silent.

"You can't expect me to believe that story," I said at last. "It's rubbish and you know it."

He raised his hand to silence me. I couldn't read his face. he was completely inscrutable then.

"No, it is not. It is true. Every word of it. As my patron insisted, I fabricated nothing."

"But it doesn't make any sense."

"True. It doesn't. Or it doesn't seem to. I returned the advance money. I *insisted* on giving it back. I had forfeited the contract. But I hadn't wasted my time. *Impressions* flooded my cortex. This sensitivity is the secret of my art. The singular atmosphere brought on a sudden blossoming of the bizarre, the necrotic, which my admirers have, well, admired. Sure, I often experienced a certain sensitivity *before* my adventure took place, but the difference, afterwards, was a whole order of magnitude."

"But how could that man be a hundred and sixty-seven? What was *going on* in that house?"

"I can only guess."

"But your *impression* – "

"Yes," said Quilt. "My impression. I learned from the driver that his master had been an artist once, or had tried to be. He was a brutal and ruthless man, very rich, but he wanted to be something more. He thought he could *take* what he wanted from nature, snatch it, like a thing off a shelf. Those were *his* paints in the closet and it was his studio in the tower room. But he failed. Perhaps he simply had no talent. Inspiration did not come. The harder he tried the more he drove himself into something like madness, beyond madness, into something altogether indescribable. Quite possibly he had achieved *gnosis*, the inner truth. He had delved too far into himself and found, in the end, only desolation. How can any of us be sure it is not the same for us?"

"What was the throwing suit?"

"I think it was a device, designed to function as it had for me. By its twistings and turnings, but the strange stresses and stranger sensations, it somehow slides the wearer outside of space and time as we know it, into – I don't know where. Wherever, he lost himself there. It was the wretched residue of his soul which I had encountered. Perhaps he too had wriggled out of the suit, but failed to catch the straps, and had fallen. Had he also crippled himself physically? I never found out. But one evening, after such experiments, he left the house forever, a changed man, utterly changed, neither dead nor alive, for he lacked an essence, whatever it is that makes us human."

I didn't know how to take this. Was Jeffrey Quilt drawing me into the most elaborate gag of all time? Or had he decided to stimulate sales by building a *mystique* around each of his paintings?

"I get it," I said. "He then went on to make a yet another pile in big business, where not having a soul was a definite advantage."

Quilt slammed his fist onto the tabletop. My beer cup hopped onto the floor and splattered.

"Forgive me," was all I could think to say.

"My purpose," he said slowly, "the reason my patron hired me, was to create a painting so effective, so vivid, so much the embodiment of the essence of that terrible place, that by staring into it he could recover his scattered soul, enough of it so that he could be human again, so he could die. I do not think he has ever succeeded, or ever will. If you don't believe me, you can ask him yourself. I'll give you his phone number. But then again, I doubt he'll want to talk about it."

We sat in silence for a while. I glanced at the painting of *The Throwing Suit*, then stared as something I couldn't define caught and held my attention.

It was only after a few minutes that I knew what I was looking at.

The picture had changed. The shrouded figure, the wearer of the throwing suit, was facing me now, its featureless mask gazing directly at me.

"Good *God*...."

"What is it?" said Quilt, alarmed.

"Nothing."

He didn't believe me, obviously. We stared at one another in silence.

"I don't understand," I said at last. "If you didn't do the painting, what is this?"

"This isn't *the* painting. I made this for myself, to commemorate the adventure." He took the painting from me, looked at it closely – I am certain he trembled slightly before he assumed a lighter, almost jovial tone and handed it back. "It's yours now. According to our bargain, you've heard the story and now you must accept the artwork."

I held it again, then looked away.

"Yours," he insisted. "You paid for it."

What terrible secret would be revealed, I wondered, when the features of that masked figure finally became clear?

"Do I have a choice?" I said after a pause.

He told me that choice didn't enter into it. Smiling sadly, more than a little drunk, he explained that Art, if it has any power at all, is revelatory and therefore it "gives knowledge; yields experiences that can't be forgotten. So in that sense there is no choice." He paused, considering something. "But I'll tell you what: if you keep the painting I'll refund your money."

Nervously, I protested, insisting he keep both the money *and* the painting.

He laughed. "That won't be necessary." Then he returned the check.

He agreed to keep *The Throwing Suit* on the strict condition that I refuse to believe the story.

"Besides," he said, shivering from the cold that I could barely feel, "there are a dozen new paintings upstairs that might interest you."

The Man in the White Mask

"**A**RGUE WITH ME, BOY!" Father screams. "Dispute! Let's hear the thunder of your words, the cannon fire of your dialectic! Say something! God – !"

He dances on the hilltop. He writhes, his brain, his soul, his very being afire with the flames of Hell. Down below, the Spanish soldiers are preparing to burn our manor house, and this desecration, this utter desolation of beautiful things gathered over the lifetimes of countless ancestors, this erasure – Yes! Especially the loss of the laboratory, where the gross elements become precious essence; and the library, where error is confounded and truth discovered, where now the very wisdom of mankind is left to perish.

These are enough to make even the non-philosopher pause and reflect on the futility that surpasses all understanding.

"Explain! Explicate! Cite chapter and verse! Damn you, I gave you a mind! Use it!" Father shrieks. He lunges at me, nearly upsetting the wheelbarrow which is my lifeboat in this shipwreck of our lives.

You gave me little else, I want to say, but I cannot find the cruelty to do so. Father stumbles. He is on his knees before me, weeping like a penitent, his hands folded in what may genuinely be prayer.

"Please be quiet," I say softly. "They'll hear us."

"They are *much* too preoccupied," he hisses back.

Profundity! Only a master painter could capture the scene, vast and dark, with suggestions of shapes, here a hill, there, far away, a town, black clouds drifting overhead with galleon slowness, and down at the bottom a spark of light as the first firebrand is raised, handed over to the bristle-chinned commander, who harumphs to the massed soldiery.

And one more thing, an enigma, an intrusion: a tall, dark, masked person stands with us on the crest of the hill, motionless. Who is he? What business has he here? I try to ask. I point. But Father will not heed. His attention is elsewhere.

"*Tercios* mercenaries," he rants, "riffraff, syphilitics. Spain's finest."

Torch light flares the commander's armor. It is infernal, this glare - worse, theatrical. Every arquebus shares the same hellish gleam, every breastplate, morion. The eyes of Spain sparkle, a field of fiends disguised as men. Pikes scratch the sky.

Now the commander, in the manner of the Sovereign Lord of Hell, bawls out a tirade long and loud in his half-incomprehensible tongue. I can barely make out the words, drifting up to me like the sound of stormy surf. A military oration.

Who can doubt their valor? Who can question the mettle of Commander Bristle-Chin as he flings the fiery torch in through the window of our steep-gabled manse? Not once does he singe himself! So deftly does Bristle-Chin accomplish his task that he ceases to seem Satanic or even militaristic. His vanity has transformed him into an acrobat, a carnival monkey drunk with his own strut. He twirls delicately. His men laugh, shaking their weapons in a demonic clatter. Evil, they say, is exquisitely banal. Perhaps this ambassador from Hell was a tumbler or a strolling player before his soldiering days.

Throughout all this time, they never notice us, though we are in plain sight, so intent are the thousands of them on their piety, their devotions, for this, too, is an *act of faith*, like so many they have performed in our country of late.

Primus. The Beginning of My Education.

On this night, for the first time, my eyes are truly opened, and I begin to read the first page in the textbook of life.

And I weep from the absurdity of it all. Not out of grief, but because I cannot laugh, and, indeed, absurdly, my conscience requires that I should be doing *something*. As I watch our house take fire, as the fire grows into a vast and living architecture of reds and oranges, I feel a deeper emotion than I have ever experienced before, something new.

Absurdity. That we stand here, alive, while Father's great library flutters away, page by page, into the night. Certainly the Spanish soldiers looted the house before burning it, but the books were of no use to them.

I call him my father, but he is not, except in the sense that God is the Father of men. No carnal act produced such a misshapen creature as myself. I am a half-finished thing of clay and human tatters, grown in a dung-heap in the traditional manner, a *homunculus* which has spent its entire existence in a wheelbarrow, shaped like a youth from the head down to the mid-chest and completely formless thereafter, without legs or bowels or manhood; animate but immobile, my lower self forever wrapped in a blanket. The fact that Father saved *me* at the end rather than dumping me out and filling the wheelbarrow with his precious books confirms my suspicion that he created me in order to have someone to argue with and lost interest as soon as I had eyes and ears and mouth and feeble arms and hands to turn pages. Now sixty, he has no one else. His wife is gone. She never had any children, for all she used to wheel me about in this conveyance claiming me as her own, just to please him. But it was too much – even she felt the terrible, agonizing absurdity; and, lacking a sense of humor, she took one last adulterous fling, then died.

"God's prank," he calls me. He says it now. "God's prank."

"No, yours," I reply.

Below, the soldiers are singing bawdy songs. How merry we all are this night!

Aged, alone, crazed enough to argue with a lump of dirt which has no particular flair for theology, this mystical and heretical arguer, Cornelius de Bloot, has needlessly risked his life too many times. Years ago his questionable experiments and Protestant extremism caused him to be imprisoned for a day and a night. He was adjured to desist. *He was warned.* Alas, the infection of his doctrines has finally cost us our pigs and chickens and our ancestral mansion...this Palace of Flame that we three refugees (Father, myself, and Odysseus the kitten, whom I cradle in my arms) now squint at.

It is a serious matter, a house-burning, the extermination of the accumulated resonances of all who have ever dwelt there. Yes, it was falling down anyway. There were no florins for repairs. The pettiest of petty nobles is my ignoble and servantless sire. Impoverished, he has lived like the most lumpish peasant, alone with the rumblings of his mind, arguing with me, his creation and mirror...wearing rustic garb patched beyond mending...with goose shit on our tables and books...while in every room he tested new heresies, exercised new schismatic theories, sought to bring about the alchemical marriage of the ethereal with the earthly; and the fumes of Hell, the teachings of Calvin and Luther, and the stinks from Father's furnace blackened the foundations long before the fires of Spain...but most of all I remember Yanna the ewe kissing me awake every morning. Dawn, viewed through Yanna's wool, was a fleecy nimbus. Never again will I smell her grass-sweet breath which made me yawn and forget, however briefly, the incompleteness of my nature.

A serious matter. These Spanish whoresons don't know how to take it seriously. They lack all rudiments of civilization.

"It is Pandemonium itself," Father sighs. "A palace of cinders."

Down below, valiant Bristle-Chin, the commander, impales a chicken on a lance – an egg-laying wonder named Peck-Peck – and hurls her into the fire. The bird squawks, *screams*, chars, her feathers going up in an explosive puff. The marauding gentlemen of Spain find this endlessly comical. Theirs is a crusade against Protestant chickens, and these sufferings are nothing compared to what torments the Devil has prepared for such heretical hens in the world to come.

I dig my nails into the sides of the wheelbarrow, stifling a scream. It is too painful, this comedy. Now Father is weeping softly, for Peck-Peck I think. By the light of Peck-Peck's demise, his teardrops are diamonds.

Not to be outdone, the other soldiers begin to toss kittens into the fire, siblings of Odysseus, whose religious opinions, likewise, are not what the Pope would want.

The commander makes another speech, completely unintelligible this time, no doubt apologizing for the meager loot: a few murdered chickens, a wheel of cheese, and Yanna, whom they will doubtless rape.

The rooftree of the house snaps thunderously, and the whole structure collapses inward, releasing constellations of swirling sparks.

Secundus. A New Chapter in the Book of My Malformed Life.

Now Odysseus, Father, and I are wanderers indeed. I have a moment of prophetic vision. I foresee him dying somewhere on a road, or in a frozen marsh, blackened, stiff, while the kitten perishes in my hands and I remain as I am, forever, neither dead nor alive, washed by seasons of rain back into my original shapelessness.

Father takes up the handles of the wheelbarrow and turns away from the holocaust. Yes, in his eyes I see bleakness and wintry wastes.

"It's all your fault," I say, loud enough for him to hear.

"My conscience is my own," he rasps back; and his face seems a pale mask, still and white as Death.

But not quite. I compare him to the *other*. I realize that the enigmatic intruder is still with us: a tall, slender figure clad in gray rags, whose serenely beautiful face is like a mask carved out of finest marble. This one nods to me from behind Father, then turns back to watch the burning.

No, Father's face is merely weary. The *other* is white as Death. I name that other *Absurdity*. That he should be mere Death, the vulgar reaper out of some ridiculous peasant mystery play, is too much. No, he is the desolator of reason, the destroyer of all order, the sublime god of nonsense, Absurdity, the only fit companion on our journey which has just begun.

But Father does not see him. Poor Father. I must make him happy if I can. I was created to argue. That is my task.

"Father, does God demand that the soldiers of Philip make their war on chickens and cats? Is it truly the God of Love who demands that so many thousands of our Dutch countrymen be 'relaxed' to the Inquisition?"

"God is good, but Satan is everywhere!" Father exclaims. For once I am inclined to agree with him. There is no argument. With surprising agility, he carts me away from the scene, till the light of the inferno behind us fades like the setting sun. I scratch Odysseus' ears so he doesn't leap out. Purrs from the kitten; a wet nose presses my palm. All at once it occurs to me that Odysseus doesn't mourn his murdered brethren at all.

"This stupid animal is completely devoid of fellow-feeling!" I declare, amazed.

Replies the August Arguer: "Only mankind possesses compassion. By God's grace we have received this treasure."

"And I, Father – ?"

"All God-fearing men are adjured to love one another, to practice compassion, to grow in Christian virtue even as – "

"Even as do the Spanish invaders consider themselves men of righteous and Godly deeds. Truly Father, we are all of us actors in some formless play of our own making. God never enters into it."

"*Blasphemy!*" cries my heretical sire as he pushes faster. Within minutes he is deep into a scathing and learned rebuttal. He doesn't need his books. He can quote, transpose, rend, distort from the library of his own mind. So heated is this diatribe that I imagine the wax melting from my ears...and after a while I pass into a kind of daze, dreaming of fire while the wheelbarrow rolls and jolts over the frozen countryside. I grieve for the kittens, for Peck-Peck. Actors, all of them, in some rambling script God left half finished, even as Father left me.... Overhead, the stars suggest freedom. The heavens are boundless, infinite. "God's mercy is infinite," I hear myself pray.

"But only for the worthy," Father pants, pushing me onward to the lightless horizon. The man in the white mask, Old Marble Face I jokingly label him, walks alongside me silently. Father cannot see him, or does not react if he does.

It is very strange.

Odysseus the kitten has slept peacefully all this while.

Tertius. Containing Life's Allegory.

Half an hour later Father is gasping for breath and we must halt at the edge of a town. A commotion nearby alerts us. Revelers, staggering drunkards. How very odd. "A *kermesse?*" I ask.

"Peasant louts. How can they go on with their merrymaking at such an hour?"

"Or in such times?"

"Political developments, I assure you, my son, never enter into the minds of these – "

A roisterous fellow with shit-stained breeches and a large, dead fish in his codpiece bumps into the wheelbarrow, rocking it. I grab hold of the kitten.

"I have been elected – " He hiccups. "– I have been elected the King of Beer. Truly, I am the heartiest guzzler of all…the very incarnation of Gambrinus…."

"Move, you clot of beer-foam! Make way for my son and myself!"

Bellows the outraged Monarch of Beer: "Why don't you throw yourself into a canal, you pillar-biting, bible-licking old turnip!"

Cursing righteously, thunderously, like Moses come down from the mountain to find the golden calf, Father turns the wheelbarrow and plunges into the sea of revelers. Their mood is, I apprehend, more desperate than truly joyous, as if only by celebration can they keep horror away. Perhaps so. Bodies collide with us from all sides. I flop backward, grab hold of the edge of the wheelbarrow, and pull myself upright once more. Odysseus, poor puss, yowls as buxom women leer and flounce their enormous breasts at us. I am amazed at the ampleness of their flesh. I only wonder how I would react if Father had made me a trifle more complete. But I can only be ashamed of my state, and play the role expected of me: a deformed beggar.

And again and again I glimpse my secret companion, the man in the white mask, flitting among the crowd, touching a whore on the shoulder, helping a sodden old man raise a stein nearly as large as he is to his lips, bumping a child backward into a rain barrel with a flourish of an elbow.

Our eyes meet, an understanding far deeper than words passes between the two of us. Suddenly we are fast friends, colleagues, fellow outcasts and outsiders.

What fools are these humans, these mortals.
Yes, holy fools, divine clowns.

I want to speak, to introduce my new-found friend to Father, but the masked one shakes his head, and is gone.

Then a fancy seizes me: we are strolling players on a tour – a cripple-thing, a crazy old man, a cat, and this *other*, who is the most brilliant of us all, the one who plays the heroic parts, handsome to the point of almost feminine beauty, lithe, strong. Here we are – set out to traverse life's gaudy stage. We whisk through a maze of celebrants and tents and trestle-tables, none too clean. Once an aged knight is with us, clad in archaic, tarnished armor like something out of an exquisite masque. He is the last hero of the Round Table, I decide, sent to find the Holy Grail here in the kingdom of the wicked, unable to die until he finds it, infinitely weary, sure to inhabit the Earth until the end of time with only myself and the Wandering Jew for company. A fancy. My fate. Drunken faces drift out of the darkness and swirling smoke. ("Cripple-bones! Beggar-legs!" If only they knew.)

We enter a forest, the babble behind us fading like the last lines of a bad play. Soon we are alone among black trees, alone with the newly risen, waning moon, with the gleaming, ice-covered branches, with the wind and the stars. From time to time I see my friend, the man in the marble-white mask, gliding between the tree trunks in utter silence. It is a comfort to have him there.

It is no more than a change of scenery, a rearrangement of the set as the play goes on, as we journey across the crowded stage – a senseless, passionate performance.

As if on cue, we reach a clearing where some genuine strolling players have pulled their wagon over by the side of the road. They laugh and wave as we pass. Such droll costumes! One woman is dressed like the crescent moon. This lunar maid throws a sugar cookie at me ("All for love!") and I catch it in my mouth like a clever dog, too polite to explain that since I have no stomach or bowels I really can't eat, and when I pretend too often the food putrefies within me and Father must pour water down my throat, shake me, and empty me out like a jug.

But, cookie in mouth, I grow wistful. Will I ever know love before I die? Will I ever truly live?

"What is life without love?" I mutter as the actors bow and curtsy.

Then one of them, a gangly angel with a gashed forehead, asks if we've seen "a man in a white mask" – a deserter from their troupe.

The cookie sticks in my throat. I cannot speak.

"No," Father replies. "What concern is it of mine if one of your fellow sinners wanders away? You will all wind up in the same place eventually. Meet him there."

The angel-actor shrugs. "Well, if you see him, run the other way, fast. He is mad. He thinks he is Grim Death himself." The actor touches his bloodied forehead. "He wields a hammer instead of a scythe, but with some skill nevertheless."

"You mock God by impersonating one of his angels," returns the Great Controversialist. "You deserve no less."

With an exaggerated bow this spindly-limbed angel bids us farewell. I am too distracted to reply. I think of my friend in the woods, pacing us on our journey for what reason I do not know. He cannot be a mere renegade actor, I am sure. That is not even absurd, merely ridiculous. The blow has addled the angel's wits, obviously.

My fantasies are too compelling for me to consider the matter further. I dream of the breasts of the moon-maid, and as I think on these shapely parts I hear a pitiful mewing and find that I'm squeezing and kneading poor Odysseus.

We pass briefly into the darkness again, through the forest, as I whisper tenderly to the frightened kitten; then we pass a haywain where, atop the haystack, two adolescents engage in fornication despite the cold. Moonlight silvers the boy's bobbing backside.

"The Devil will send them a letter of thanks," my cheerless Father says. I stifle a laugh. Then I regard myself with amazement. The excitement of the night, the stimulus, all this motion have changed me. I am becoming more human. How much I yearn for such Satanic commendations, Father can never know.

Onward. I look to left and to right for my friend in the white mask. I want to share my discovery with him. But there are only the black trees, passing one by one in the darkness.

Scant minutes later we overtake an old Jew clad in a skullcap and patchwork cloak. He falls in beside us. He warns us that Leyden Town swarms with pro-Spanish *Glippers*. Flanders is in decline, he says. The seaports are silting up, and Royalist atrocities occur daily. He identifies himself as an Antwerper, a follower of Erasmus. ("That bloated bladder of Humanistic pap!" opines my father, but the Jew only smiles.) Before he leaves us, this worthy son of Abraham warns us that the Spanish seek two fugitives, a *de vehementi* dogmatizer and his crippled son.

A little while later, in a field where corpses still smolder at a dozen stakes, Father and I pause to consider this description of ourselves. I wonder if fire would merely harden me like a piece of pottery, since I am made of clay, not flesh. But then Scripture clearly states that Adam and the sons of Adam were likewise made from clay.

Yet this woman-borne clay does not harden. Even as we linger there, one of the corpses emits a noise. I raise a hand to my mouth to stifle a cry. But the corpse merely shifts in its scorched bonds, throwing sparks, like a log settling in a fireplace.

Heretics all.

Startled by our intrusion, sleeping crows awake and caw at us. They are waiting for morning, when their breakfast will be cooled enough to eat.

"We must find shelter," Father says. "We cannot go on. We must rest." But I don't want to rest. For all the loss of the house has pained me, for all the deaths of the chickens and cats have filled me with horror, the night has been an exciting one, filled with so many new sights and sounds and experiences. I am like a baby newborn, eager to be alive for the first time.

Absurdity. Beautiful absurdity.

He wheels me away. I glance back and see the man in the white mask standing among the charred corpses. Our eyes meet.

Soon, he says. *I shall join you very soon.*

Quartus. In Which Base Imposture Is Transmuted Into Golden Truth.

When we reach a certain furrowed field used as a mass grave by the Spaniards, Father announces that we are safe. No one comes there at night for fear of the countless, outraged ghosts of the slain. We will be safe there, for we, too, are outraged.

It is a great, frozen stewpot of a place, filled with bodies imperfectly buried. Limbs and heads jut from the earth. Armor and helmets glint in the moonlight. Old rusty pikes stand like a flourish of malnourished trees.

"How many Netherlanders lie here?" I ask, trying to be casual.

"God knows." Father taps the soil with his foot. "This is a crowded place. Soldiers of Orange, Walloons, victims of the Inquisition, some Spaniards, German mercenaries. Plague corpses. Thousands upon thousands."

"The Triumph of Death," I hear myself remark, not really understanding what that means. Since I am not truly alive, how can I understand death? A vexing problem. Father and I will thrash it out sometime. But now –

Odysseus leaps from my lap, runs over to a leathery hand protruding from the soil, sniffs, and meows mournfully.

"We must pray for these poor souls," Father says.

And I wonder, too, whether or not a homunculus like myself even has a soul. I suspect not. I have more in common with Odysseus the kitten than with Cornelius de Bloot.

But he created me as an arguer:

"What good will your prayers do for the Dead? I say, let the living pray for the living!"

(Well argued, clay-thing. Where does that leave you, homuncular lump? I have no idea.)

"Such disrespect!"

I reach out my hand. Odysseus returns to my lap. "You and your valueless prayers. Think how much happier mankind would be if nobody prayed, ever. There would be fewer heretic-fueled fires lit in this world." I am momentarily sentimental, stroking the cat. My eyes well up with teardrops; I see a blurry vision of Father opening and closing his mouth.

"You are no longer my son," says this watery replica after a few seconds.

"Was I ever?"

Father roars. I hurl the cat at his chest. Not to be outdone, he snaps off an arm from the frozen corpse of a *Schwartzreiter* pistoleer and whacks me across the shoulder with it. Odysseus scrambles for safety among a heap of skulls. Soon Father and I are pelting one another with clods of earth – I nearly spill myself reaching for more ammunition – and throughout the battle there is laughter from an intermediate distance.

A stranger, dressed in a cassock of indescribable blackness.

"Ho there," says he as Father flings a heavy boot at my ear.

"Whoever you are, the affairs of a father and his son are no concern of yours," the great theologian Cornelius de Bloot shouts in his most exasperated manner.

Heavy silence. Then the black-cassocked man in the crudely carved, wooden skull mask steps forward. He is but a ludicrous caricature of that fascinating *other*. "But this is my domain." The stranger's voice through the mask is soft, silken, infinitely reasonable. "I am the *Stadholder* of this melancholy place."

Stammers Father: "Some *Stadholder*.... Who are you and why do you wear that ridiculous mask?"

"Lo, I am the Pontiff of Despair; and my throne is the throne of woe. I lead you now into the infernal city. Abandon all hope – "

Father snorts derisively.

"But your droll behaviors have cheered me somewhat," the stranger goes on. "Yonder is the *sanctum sanctorum* of my realm." He points to a heap of charred bones. "I yearn for such entertainers as yourselves; for my palace is hollow with echoes and lacks mirth."

"We are not strolling players!"

I point to the wooden mask and proclaim like a child who is being very clever, "I know you!"

"All men know of me in the end," comes the sepulchral reply, "but few seek me before their appointed time. Tell me, what brings you both into this darkness?"

Father clears his throat, as if about to make a speech. "I am Cornelius de Bloot, truth's dearest martyr, unafraid to lay bare my mind whatever the consequence! This runty baggage is my son, Adam."

"Very droll indeed!" (Can he possibly know? Is he going to count my ribs?) "A bag of nettles, your son. It seems he does not share your theological views."

This pretend-Death waves a white-gloved hand and begins to walk away. Father hefts the wheelbarrow and follows.

I call out, "Even so, we are both fugitives, heretical opinions being our alleged crime."

"You are betrayers, betrayed," the man in the wooden mask laughs. "But this sits well with me. It really does; for I am out of sorts with the tenor of the times and all religious disputes confound me. So tell me, Adam de Bloot, are you a Calvinist or a Catholic?"

Here is a sublime absurdity indeed. I am my Father's mirror. I am an answerer, the lesser end of an endless dialogue in flesh and clay. I never thought of myself as actually holding a position –

"My beliefs are a personal matter."

Again, Father snorts. He huffs for breath. Surely the adventures of the night have fatigued him to his utmost limit.

"Yet you walk the same heretical path as your father," the masked impostor goes on, ignoring him.

I glance down at the blanket in my lap. Odysseus should be curled there asleep, but he is not. I don't know what has become of him. "I walk nowhere – It is only this affliction which binds me to my father and his opinions."

"Yes, but are you a Lutheran or Loyalist, Calvinist or Catholic?"

Ah, the banality of evil! For an instant I shudder, afraid this man is no more than an informer, an agent of the secret police. But I reject the notion as insufficiently fantastic.

"My son doesn't know which end he shits out of," Father gasps. (Exquisite! Droll, yes!)

Again the question floats from behind the crude wooden mask: *"What are you, Adam de Bloot?"*

"I don't know what I am," I hear myself answer.

"Truth is a sly response," the cassocked one laughs into my face, leaning so low that I can feel his hot breath through the mouth-hole of the mask. He stands up and continues his discourse. "Calvinists and Catholics. Both sects are committed to purely spiritual values. What a marvel that they fight like wild beasts in this purely material world. Ah well. Folly reigns over all."

He laughs at my father now, who seems exhausted of words and only turns his face away.

"Follow me to my castle. There, Cornelius de Bloot, we shall engage in learned conversation. What theories we may spin. We shall immerse our intellects in a sea of debates, and know the true and inner natures of God and Satan and Mankind. Let us sup on controversy. Let us gorge ourselves on dialectic – "

"And puke up – " But Father cannot think of any clever ending, and leaves the phrase dangling.

The other ignores this sudden and inexplicable failure of vocabulary in the Great Arguer. "What say you, Cornelius de Bloot?"

"Do you mock me?" is all Father can reply. Truly age and weariness have taken their toll.

"I offer you freedom from *this!*" The black-robed figure gestures quite dramatically to the mounds of corpses. I follow the sweep of his hand. Filling my gaze are the armies of the night, very still. "I offer you more than mere hospitality. An intellectual, spiritual haven awaits you."

"Ah," says Father. "We shall see what we shall see."

Absurdity! Priceless!

Quintus. Which Concludes Endearingly.

"We have come, at last," says the man in the white wooden mask. (How primitive the workmanship of that mask – it looks like an enormous nutshell vaguely carved into a travesty of a human face, then painted white. It would frighten only an imbecile.) "...to the heart of my empire, the very Castle of Unease, where we shall be nevertheless at our ease to dispute and wrangle and pull the truth out of falsehood like torturers with our tongs – or should I say tongues?"

He seems to pause as if awaiting applause for this feeble play on words, but neither Father nor I heed him. We are too amazed at what we see.

It is a Castle of Unease indeed. It must have taken the madman months to construct. How, then, could he have deserted his fellow players only this night? Perhaps he sneaked away on regular intervals to work on this imperial project. Or else thousands upon thousands of lunatics have labored here and died, adding their bones to the already impressive collection, contributing themselves to the very masonry.

The structure is a supernatural manifestation, surely, not the work of this self-deluded trespasser, but of a far, far greater architect.

Upended coffins form the walls. Human bones fill in the gaps, jut from the tops to form the battlements. A gate of cunningly joined bones swings in the night breeze. In silence, we three enter. (Where is Odysseus the kitten? I never do find out. No matter. He does not belong. Cats are never absurd.) Within, the facade of the Palace of Woe is even more incredible. Thousands of skulls, neatly arranged, grin down at us, forming windows, arches, walls. Twisted metal writhes among them, like wrought-iron ivy. The faint wind sings as it passes through. Moonlight gleams on bare bone, on frost, on ice.

In the center of a single, round chamber, the masked one takes his seat on a throne of human remains, whole bodies obviously thawed and shaped and refrozen into truly demented positions. Behind, hundreds of arms rise up like fronds. Before, skeletons lie on the floor in supplication. On either side, frozen pikemen in finest armor stand a guard of honor.

Father maneuvers the single wheel of my conveyance through human debris, crunching ribs, femurs, vertebrae.

"Father," I whisper, "I beg you. No more arguments, no more contradictions. Take us both away from here."

"I can only go forward," he says, "never back."

"Never back!" thunders our host, who has overheard our conversation.

"Besides," Father says meekly, "he has offered us shelter."

This is not absurdity now. It is not delicious, exhilarating. There is no trace of the imaginative in it. It is merely dreary humiliation, the pain of old age. The events of the night have broken my father's spirit. I resolve to arouse him, to make him whole once more, before it is too late and our mad guest loses patience with the uninspired dialectic.

Forward. Above and around me, the universe spirals on its crazed path to some unknown end. But before me, a new horror. The wooden-masked one works some kind of lever, and a section of the floor slides away to reveal an open coffin, and there, peacefully composed, *is the corpse of the moon-maiden actress*, still in her amusing costume, her huge and fascinating breasts bare, frozen solid like curves of ivory. Only her forehead is marred by a congealed wound.

"I am king of this land," announces our host. "It is only fitting that I have a queen. Is it not so? Now dispute with me, Cornelius de Bloot!"

"I – "

"Come now! Deliberate! Explicate! Do something! Give me some words! What of freedom of conscience? Should laity read the scriptures? What of the two wills, divine and human, or is it just one? Is the Pope the successor to Peter or is he the Great Beast? Tell me!"

He leans forward on his hideous throne. For an instant it seems that there is nothing behind his mask at all except perhaps a faint candle flame. Then I am truly afraid, that this impersonator is not the real impostor at all, not the mad, renegade actor, but a *thing of spirit* –

I reach for his mask, but it is too far, of course. Father swats my hands down. To the Lord of Woe he says, "Sir, I think you insult me. Have a care."

"Better...Yes, better...but still it lacks fire. *Seigneur* de Bloot, a man of your erudition should not be ashamed to air his views *fully* and at *great length*...."

"As indeed I am not," says Father, suddenly standing rigidly upright, like a soldier at attention. Then he slumps again. "But I am very tired."

Oh, it is a pity, an agony, to see my father reduced thus! First and above all else he is an arguer, a debater, a thunderer of logic and invective. For him to fail, now, for him to *fail to appreciate the absurdity of our situation,* for him to express nothing at all in the face of this ludicrous fraud is more than the heart – even the clay heart – can bear. It is, yes, like death.

Our host, too, is disappointed. He descends from his throne. Something, a rat perhaps, scurries among the bones. Father falls to his knees in utter exhaustion, his hands folded, but he cannot pray. He is beyond even that. He gazes blankly at the frozen corpse of the actress.

The masked one walks among the rubbish by the edge of the open grave. He removes a blood-stained mallet from beneath his cassock, raises it to strike.

"Father!" I cry. "Father! *I have ceased to believe in God!*"

And he is himself again! He rises. He thunders. *"What?"* I repeat my fantastic charge; and, roaring like some enraged bull, he lunges at me. The mallet-stroke goes wild. Father and I tumble, wheelbarrow and all, into the grave, onto the frozen breasts of the moon-maiden.

Then Father is shouting, and the would-be Grim Reaper is hauling him up out of the grave by the ankles. I can barely move, so puny are my arms, so useless the distorted mass of my body. I lie on my back, atop my beloved moon-maiden, and flail my limbs uselessly in the air. But up above me, the battle is magnificent, as Father's opinions and deliberations and quotations of Holy Writ are like a cannonade, like a raging tempest, and his opponent can only stutter and squeal and bark like a dog while the two of them grapple, mind-to-mind, hand-to-hand. There's a wondrous glimpse of Father with his hands around the impostor's neck, the wooden mask askew, the face beneath an explosion of protruding eyes and tongue and inferior scholarship.

Ah Father!

*   *   *

It is only much later that, slowly, painfully, I wriggle out of the grave like some crippled worm, my hands bloody, my arms and shoulders all but screaming from the exertion.

I pause, wheezing, my breath coming in opaque puffs. Otherwise the room is silent. The darkness of the night has faded into the gray of first light.

There I espy the forms of the crazed impostor, dead, his neck broken, and Father, likewise dead and glassy-eyed, heaved backward by the dying man's last desperate effort, dangling three feet above the floor, impaled on a pike held by one of the frozen corpse-guards.

The impostor's face is quite ordinary, craggy and unshaven.

Then something moves. I turn with effort and behold the man in the white mask, the true one, my companion of the road. He glides over the corpse-and-bone rubble like a cloud. He bows before me. His mask is more beautiful, more delicately featured than I have ever seen it before. It glows from within, as if the pale sun is rising inside his head.

"You are *Absurdity!*" I croon. "You are the spirit of all things incongruous. You are the ruler of our age!" There, I have said it. It is my first, my only original opinion. I am no mere foil for Father's arguments now.

The other is startled. He shakes his head, sadly. I swear it. Sadly.

"I am Death," he says. "Did you not know me? I am the messenger of endings."

"No, you are absurd. Life is likewise absurd. You cannot be Death; Death makes perfect sense!"

"Does it?" He touches Father's face, closing his frozen eyes. "Does absurdity then make perfect sense?"

I lack any reply. Were this a debate, he would be the victor.

"I am your admirer! Your disciple!" Even as I say it, I don't know what that means. The words merely come.

"Yes," he says. "You are."

Miracle of miracles: Death himself gives me life, for he has stolen so many and can surely spare one for a little while. He shapes me with his cold hands, forming the lower part of my body in every detail, fashioning legs and feet, helping me upright, explaining to me as he works that I have been able to see him all this while because I was neither truly alive nor dead, whereas human beings may only glimpse him at the appointed hour, when their doom is upon them. I, lump of clay, vegetable product of a dung-heap, *homunculus*, have therefore been a visionary, a kind of prophet. My eyes have been open all along, while those of men remained closed. I have seen far more deeply into the nature of things than any other.

But now I have become a man, and this vision fades. I can barely discern him at all, only a suggestion of shadow, a movement like a wisp of smoke, and the glowing white mask floating in the air, illuminating the gloomy interior of the bone-palace.

His whisper is like the wind. "Now, go forth, my creation, my ally, and live truly as men live. You are strong. You are lustful. You shall seize riches and lands, and be reckoned great among your kind. You shall send many into my kingdom, as tribute. Go now, and the world shall tremble at your tread. Go."

I pull the impostor's cassock off his body to cover my nakedness, and go.

Much later, at the edge of the death-fields, I look back. Mist rises out of the frozen earth at the touch of the sun. I see them for a moment, heading in solemn, silent procession back into the fading night, into the dark lands: Death in his glowing white mask, bearing an hourglass and a scythe; and the impostor, crestfallen and penitent in his underwear with his crude mask dangling from his neck; the actress with her moon-shaped costume and naked breasts; and Father, animate, waving his arms, leaping up and down, *arguing* furiously, shouting theology, dialectic, all manner of heresy no doubt – *arguing* with Death himself.

He is magnificent, my Father, and definitely absurd. At this moment I love him very much.

About Jason Van Hollander, Darrell Schweitzer writes: I encountered Jason Van Hollander in a writing class about 1986, which sounds pretty arrogant, because he knew about himself all along. I was just slow on the uptake. Nevertheless, I've since discovered him to be an enormously talented artist, whose work has graced the pages of many issues of Weird Tales, *not to mention various Tor and Arkham House books. His fiction is not inconsiderable. Look for his solo stories in* Marion Zimmer Bradley's Fantasy Magazine #6 *and* Weird Tales #302. *His fiction is even weirder than mine, which is why we work so well together. He can bring out things even I never suspected I had in me. He lives in a cosy house in Merion, PA with numerous toy robots, many paintings, and his lovely (and also talented) wife Terry, who puts up with both of us.*

Of Darrell, Jason writes: I was honored but a little mystified when, in 1986, Darrell suggested that we collaborate on a story. Our ideas and styles meshed; we were pleased with the result. Eventually six of our published collaborations were given honorable mentions in THE YEAR'S BEST FANTASY AND HORROR, *(ed. by Ellen Datlow and Terri Windling, St. Martin's Press). Darrell and his wife Mattie live in a gigantic book repository that contains, among other things, cats, furniture, a miniature dance floor, and, one assumes, two or three out-of-tune ukuleles.*